THE MYTHICAL 9th DIVISION

THE MAGMA CONSPIRACY

ALEX MILWAY

Kane Miller
A DIVISION OF EDC PUBLISHING

For Saskia

First American Edition 2013
Kane Miller, A Division of EDC Publishing

Copyright © 2011 Alex Milway

For information contact:
Kane Miller, A Division of EDC Publishing
PO Box 470663
Tulsa, OK 74147-0663
www.kanemiller.com
www.edcpub.com
www.usbornebooksandmore.com

Library of Congress Control Number: 2012948538

Printed and bound in the United States of America
2 3 4 5 6 7 8 9 10
ISBN: 978-1-61067-159-0

www.mythical9thdivision.com

FOR 150 YEARS A *MYSTERIOUS* TRIO OF HEROIC AND RESOURCEFUL YETIS HAS EXISTED AS A *TOP-SECRET* BRANCH OF THE BRITISH ARMED FORCES. OVER THE YEARS, SUCCESSIVE GENERATIONS OF YETIS HAVE WORKED FEARLESSLY TO DEFEND THE WORLD AGAINST *THE FORCES OF EVIL*. AS THESE POWERS GROW EVER DEADLIER, THE YETIS FIGHT ON, PITTING BOTH *STRENGTH* AND *WITS* AGAINST THE MIGHT OF THEIR ENEMIES.

THEY ARE THE MYTHICAL 9TH DIVISION.

NO SMOKE WITHOUT FIRE

Fears are growing over increased seismic activity at Mount Vesuvius, one of the most dangerous volcanoes in the world. With around three million humans living in its shadow, a full scale eruption, like that in AD 79 which destroyed Pompeii, could be devastating.

Local scientists and volcanologists are monitoring the volcano's emissions and will hopefully be able to predict when a full eruption might take place.

Chapter 1: McMurdo

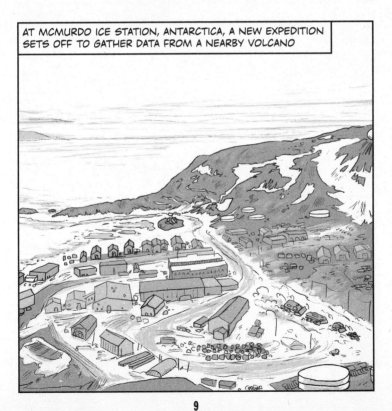

AT MCMURDO ICE STATION, ANTARCTICA, A NEW EXPEDITION SETS OFF TO GATHER DATA FROM A NEARBY VOLCANO

FOUR WEEKS LATER, THE SUNLESS ANTARCTIC WINTER HAS SET IN...

AND ALBRECHT AND SAAR ARE ON A MISSION

The winter wind blew hard and cold across Antarctica as a snowstorm raged, making passage across the Ross Ice Shelf impossible for a human.

For a yeti, however, it was a walk in the park.

"It's nice and warm today," said Saar, loosening the scarf around his neck. "It's almost a shame we're on a mission."

"I'm worried about Timonen, though..." said Albrecht. "I knew it was a bad idea letting him walk off by himself."

"Timonen only cares about his belly," replied Saar.

"Well, he's not going to find much to eat out there," said Albrecht, "unless he wants ice cubes for breakfast."

He rubbed a clump of hardened snow from his eyebrows and looked through his binoculars. The orange glow of McMurdo Ice Station shone out like a beacon in the storm.

"If he doesn't hurry up," added Albrecht, "I might have to

have a few words with him."

"If you write them on his eyeballs, they may sink in," said Saar. And with each step aided by the Staff of Ages, the wise yeti trudged on with a smile on his face. "If only all days were like this," he said.

Albrecht was about to reply when something caught his attention and he stopped briefly. He peered into the darkness, sniffed the air and rubbed his ears.

"Can you hear a grumbling sound?" he asked.

Saar pushed the fur from his ears and listened closely to the howling wind.

"I can," he said. "It's getting louder..."

"And closer," said Albrecht. He paused.

Moments later, a giant snowball blasted straight into the two surprised yetis. They vanished into its tumbling icy heart, rolling across the ice sheet at incredible speed.

"WAAAAAAAAAAAH!" cried Albrecht, spinning over and over like a giant furry rug in an enormous washing machine.

"Hold on!" shouted Saar.

"I feel sick!" cried Albrecht.

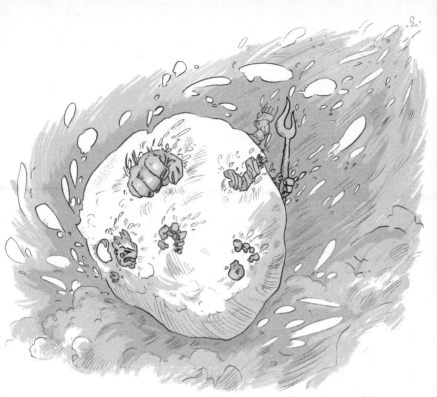

The snowball hit a ridge of volcanic rock and soared into the air like a meteor, before crashing down in the center of McMurdo Ice Station.

Snow and yetis flew everywhere.

"Albrecht?" spluttered Saar. "Would you please take your foot off my face."

Albrecht coughed and spat out a mouthful of snow.

"I was going to ask you to do the same," he said.

"But my feet are nowhere near—"

Both yetis fell silent.

"Morning," said Timonen.

The huge yeti groaned as he forced himself onto his feet. His eyes were swimming in their sockets.

"Quite a ride!" he said, stepping back shakily. "Where are we?"

"You!" said Saar. "You always get us into trouble!"

"Wait a minute!" said Timonen, rubbing his eyes. "I didn't plan this."

"That's the problem," said Saar. "You never plan anything. It's lucky for us there's a snowstorm and all the humans are tucked away indoors."

"Now, now, let's not argue," said Albrecht, rising to his feet and brushing his fur free of snow. "We need to find our contact before the storm clears."

He switched on his RoAR to access a map of the area.

"This way," he said, and set off through the snowy streets.

Saar pulled himself upright and marched after him.

Timonen brought up the rear.

"Who is it we're meeting?" asked Timonen.

"Were you listening to a word Albrecht said at the briefing?" said Saar.

"Of course not," said Timonen. "I was hungry."

"That's it!" said Saar. "Don't speak to me again."

"Really?" said Timonen. "Please tell me you really mean it?"

"I mean it," he replied angrily.

"Wonderful," said Timonen. "I'll talk to Albrecht instead. Where are we going?"

"We're delivering a package to a scientist," he said wearily.

"Will this scientist have food?" said Timonen.

"I assume so," said Albrecht.

"That's all I need to know – just show me the way."

As the yetis navigated the wide snowbound streets, they could see the tips of snowmobiles poking out of the snow beside each building. They passed a series of huge dome-like containers and then came to a much smaller blue structure, which resembled an aircraft hangar.

"That's the place," said Albrecht, pointing to it.

He strode to the door and scooped away the pile of snow that blocked the entrance. Albrecht pressed a red button on the keypad labeled INTERCOM, and after a moment's pause, a squeaky voice crackled out of a speaker.

"Who is it?" said the voice. "This had better be important – I'm not coming out there in this weather for just anyone."

"Um … right…" stuttered Albrecht, remembering his code name. "It's Snowman Alpha. With Snowmen Beta and Gamma."

"Oh!" replied the voice. "Now that changes everything. Just give me a second to gear up."

Albrecht looked puzzled.

"Do you know who this person is?" asked Saar.

"No idea," said Albrecht. "All I know is he's a top-secret LEGENDS operative."

After a short wait, the yetis heard a quiet clunk which seemed to come from the direction of Albrecht's knees. They looked down. A very small hatch had opened at the base of the door.

"My, you're huge!" said a tiny man who'd appeared at Albrecht's feet.

He was wrapped in thick weatherproof gear and his only defining features were a rosy red face and large nose that burst forth from his hood.

"And he's never going to fit through the door," the little man continued, pointing to Timonen.

"A mouse wouldn't fit through *that* door," said Timonen.

The man grew angry and clenched his fists.

"If you're going to be rude you can stay out here in the freezing cold!"

"Like I care," said Timonen.

"That'll do," said Albrecht. He knelt down and lowered his head to the floor to look at the man eye to eye. "We've brought your special package."

The man's expression changed in an instant to one of glee. He rubbed his gloved hands and dashed off through the door.

"Well, don't just stand there," he shouted over his shoulder. "Come in! Come in!"

Albrecht looked at Saar, who looked at Timonen, who looked at the impossibly small door the man had disappeared through.

"Through there?" said Saar.

Seconds later, the main door opened with a loud *clang*.

"Hurry up! The snow's getting in!" said the man.

It was still a squeeze, but with much holding of breath the three yetis made it through the entrance and the door sealed shut behind them.

The warmth hit them immediately, as did the sight before them.

"It's like Santa's Grotto," said Timonen tactlessly.

The yetis were standing at the edge of a sprawling miniature laboratory. Platforms led off from the main walkway, joined by stairwells made for tiny feet. The building was packed with tiny scientific equipment and tiny computers, all operated by a team of tiny people. Machines ticked away in the background, LEDs flashed on and off and strange liquids bubbled in glass jars.

"Take a seat," said the man, directing them towards a set of chairs perfect for a yeti-sized dollhouse.

"No," said Albrecht to Timonen, who was about to demolish one with his little finger. "Use your brain…"

"What a ridiculous thing to say," muttered Saar.

"So where is it?" asked the little man, ignoring the bickering.

Albrecht unstrapped his backpack and withdrew a small metal tin, no larger than a matchbox. He passed it to the man.

"Excuse my ignorance," said Saar, "but are you a gnome?"

"Of course," he said, placing the tin on the table. "I'm Grubchook, a secret operative of the Mythical 7th Division, but if you tell anyone I'll have to silence you."

"Ooh, scary," said Timonen.

"See this, yeti?" said Grubchook, stretching over the table and picking up a gnome-sized jug of brown liquid. "This will burn a hole through steel," he said. "Imagine what it'll do to your feet."

Timonen wisely retreated.

"I'm pretty sure that smells like coffee," whispered Saar to Albrecht, "but he doesn't need to know."

Grubchook opened the tin and his eyes glowed with excitement. He held its contents aloft: it was a square computer cartridge.

"Finally I can log on to the mainframe!" he said, disappearing behind a bank of computers.

Timonen yawned with boredom. The computers booted up, revealing an image of a globe crisscrossed by bright lines.

"With the new software I'll be able to access all LEGENDS databases from the comfort of my own lab!" said Grubchook, reappearing by Albrecht's feet.

"We came all this way for *that*?" said Timonen.

"Are you always this stupid?" said Grubchook. "Do you know what would happen if this fell into enemy hands? Watch!"

He typed a few commands into a computer, and the screens flashed up live shots of the yowies of the Mythical 5th Division. Grubchook had tapped into surveillance cameras in Blue Base canteen.

"Hey!" said Albrecht. "That's Cob eating a burger."

"Don't remind me of those," said Timonen.

"That's amazing," said Saar. "So you can interact with all the divisions now?"

"Exactly," said Grubchook. "All my data and findings can be accessed by everyone else. We're one big family."

"There's nothing big about you," said Timonen.

"Remember hot, burning acid melting through your feet," said Grubchook.

Timonen fell silent.

"So what do you gnomes do here?" asked Albrecht.

"We keep an eye on the environment," said Grubchook. "We monitor changes in climate and weather systems, as well as tectonic plate movements and volcanic emissions."

The gnome continued to test out the new capabilities of his computer. He ran through reams of data, scanned through photos of tropical creatures and then chanced upon some schematics of an alien spacecraft.

"Ooh," he said, "nice."

"So how is the environment these days?" said Saar.

"Doomed," said Grubchook. He was about to launch into an explanation when a gnome appeared at the end of the walkway, running towards them fast.

"Emergency!" he gasped, as he dragged Grubchook away by the arm.

"Stay where you are," Grubchook shouted to the yetis. He rushed down the walkway and scooted up a different flight of stairs to meet a group of gnomes huddled in front of a monitor.

"Looks serious," said Saar, watching from afar.

Within a minute, Grubchook was back.

"Our underground monitors show there's a disturbance in the Terror Rift," he said. "This snowstorm has impeded our cameras, but I'm almost certain that Mount Erebus is erupting."

"The volcano?" said Albrecht.

"We're not directly in danger," said Grubchook, "but it may disrupt your journey home."

Another gnome rushed to Grubchook's side.

"Sir, I've just heard that there's a research team still out at Erebus," she said. "If they aren't rescued quickly, they won't stand a chance!"

"We can't do anything in these conditions," said Grubchook. "It would take us weeks to navigate the snow with our legs."

"Are there many in the team?" asked Albrecht.

"Ten, maybe twenty," said the gnome.

"It sounds like we should we go and help?" suggested Saar.

"You're certainly much better built for these emergencies,"

said Grubchook. "But it would be incredibly dangerous."

Timonen patted Albrecht on the back, winding him.

"Come on," he said. "I've never seen a volcano erupt!"

"All right," said Albrecht, coughing. "Let's do it."

"First things first, though," said Timonen. "I need to eat. What have you got, gnome?"

Grubchook looked at the massive yeti and retrieved a tiny sandwich from a vending machine.

"Here you go," said the gnome, laughing. "Rations are short."

Timonen picked up the sandwich between his thumb and forefinger. It was the size of a penny at best.

"You call that a sandwich?" he said. "I call that a crumb!"

"Not only do you have a cavernous mouth," said Grubchook, "but it's obvious you have a cavernous stomach, too."

Timonen stomped to the door.

"Open up," he said angrily. "I'll get a warmer welcome from that volcano than I'll get here."

THE MYTHICAL 9th DIVISION

Chapter 2: Fire and Ice

THE YETIS HEAD OUT INTO THE COLD

IT SHOULD BE EASY TO FIND AN ERUPTING VOLCANO.

28

KRAKKK!!!

"I can't imagine the research team will last long out here," said Saar.

The volcano was in the midst of a full, terrifying eruption and the landscape was lit a fiery fiendish red. Lumps of red-hot lava rocketed through the air and Albrecht threw himself into the snow as one smashed down beside him.

"If these fireballs get any worse," he said, "we'll be burned to a crisp, never mind them!"

The plume of smoke from the crater grew blacker by the second, heightened by the glowing red bile spewing from its mouth. "It's a death zone!" said Saar.

Albrecht rose to his feet and surveyed the area with his binoculars. Searching the volcano for survivors was difficult when he had to keep one eye on the sky for lava bombs.

"I can see three vehicles," he said, zooming in. "They look like tanks."

The vehicles glowed green through his night-vision setting.

"Yeah, three large snow tanks," he said. "Looks like they've been cut off by the lava."

"Sounds tricky," said Saar.

A cluster of lava bombs smashed into the ground nearby, covering the yetis in slush.

"This may be beyond us," said Saar, wiping his face.

"Don't be such a wimp," said Timonen. "What this needs is a super yeti!"

He rushed off through the storm.

"Here we go again," said Albrecht. "Wait up!"

Ducking and diving the fireballs that whizzed overhead, the yetis edged nearer to the lava flow. Before long they could see faint lights glowing on the snow tanks. The vehicles were trapped on a rocky outcrop, with lava creeping past them on either side. A few humans were bustling around, beaming flashlights at the lava.

"They're panicking," said Saar.

The yetis ran faster until they were halfway up the grumbling volcano. They stopped at the edge of the lava flow and looked at the stranded vehicles a few hundred yards away.

"There's no way across," said Albrecht.

"Can't we just walk through it?" said Timonen.

"Depends on whether you want to keep your feet or not," said Saar. "We need to think. Maybe try getting their attention?"

"So this stuff's hot?" said Timonen, bending down to sniff the lava.

His nose was just inches from the molten rock when Albrecht dragged him back.

"Do you have to be so stupid?" he shouted.

"What?" said Timonen. "You have to try things!"

"Yes and you try my patience."

"Oh my goodness," said Saar. "Look!"

The humans had returned to their vehicles, and among the swirling smoke and fire, the tanks had started to move.

"What are they doing?" said Saar. "Tank tracks can't withstand that heat – they'll melt! They'll be burned alive!"

It was too late. The vehicles slipped off the outcrop and into the lava.

"No!" shouted Albrecht, chasing around the edge of the lava flow.

Nothing could stop the vehicles, and surprisingly this counted for the lava, too. It was having absolutely no effect on the tanks.

"How can they keep going?" said Saar, as the tanks reached the edge of the sea of lava and traveled out onto the cooler ground with ease. "The lava should have melted that metal."

"There's something fishy going on here," said Albrecht. "Let's get to the bottom of this."

The yetis chased off at full speed after the snow tanks. The ground started to shake below them.

"What now?" said Albrecht, kneeling down.

"Earthquake?" said Saar, clutching his staff to steady himself.

"It's right underneath me!" yelled Timonen, arms wind-milling as the snow erupted beneath his feet. He was thrown backwards as a gigantic drill burst through the ground and appeared between his legs.

The other two yetis scurried to safety as a huge tank, conical drill at its front, made its way out of the mountainside. Apart from the drill, the vehicle looked just like the other snow tanks they'd seen.

"Well," said Albrecht, sitting upright amidst a blast of exhaust fumes. "I wasn't expecting that!"

Timonen jumped up and punched the vehicle.

"What are you playing at?" he roared, smashing his fists hard into its sides. They didn't even dent the surface.

"Look!" said Saar, pointing to an insignia on the side of the tank. "Magma Corps."

Albrecht grabbed his backpack and searched frantically for his RoAR.

"Can't you hear me?!" shouted Timonen, now sitting on the tank and hammering the roof to no avail. "What are you doing?!"

As if in answer, the engine roared aloud, then with a loud squeal, a panel beneath Timonen flipped upwards and threw him to the snow.

Out of the tank rose a figure, clothed in a red, all-weather snowsuit. On his face was a sinister black metal welding mask with an orange rectangular panel at its center. It was focused on the yetis. Fireballs continued to rain down, the blaze of their burning trails illuminating the man in the tank. He surveyed the scene slowly and ominously, taking a long time over the yetis.

Albrecht's RoAR flashed brightly, capturing a photo of the man before he vanished back into the tank and closed the panel. With a growl from the engine the tank powered off across the snow, leaving the yetis alone and confused.

"I must have scared him off," said Albrecht, looking nervously at the lava bubbling out of a hole in the ground near his feet.

"Don't be ridiculous," laughed Timonen. "If anything scared him it was my fists."

"Of all the times for a discussion," said Saar, attempting to push Timonen down the slope with his staff, "this isn't it. Let's go before we sizzle to death."

"You're such a scaredy-cat," said Timonen, digging in his heels.

"I told you never to talk to me again," said Saar.

Albrecht could feel the heat from the lava warming his face.

"Saar's right," he said. "Let's get back to McMurdo and find out more about that research team…"

"Oh, not the gnomes again," said Timonen.

Albrecht forced the big yeti into action.

"Move," he said, shoving him in the back. "I, for one, will be glad when we're away from here."

Back at McMurdo Ice Station, the yetis bundled into Grubchook's laboratory.

"It's the worst eruption since records began," said Grubchook, hurrying them in. His fellow gnomes were frantically trying to measure the effects of the eruption with their scientific instruments.

"Did you rescue them?" he asked.

"They didn't need our help," said Albrecht.

"What?"

"They could drive through the lava," said Saar. "And drill through the ground."

"They were drilling into the volcano?" said Grubchook.

"That's most unsafe. That could cause an—"

"Eruption?" said Albrecht. "That's what I thought. It would explain why you didn't get any warning signals."

"This research team – Magma Corps," said Saar. "You know of them?"

Grubchook scratched his chin. "Not me, no," he said.

He walked to his computer and accessed the station logs.

"There's no record of them before their recent arrival," said Grubchook. "And where did they go after they escaped the lava?"

"No idea," said Albrecht.

"We lost track of them on the ice shelf," said Saar. "It wasn't safe to follow them."

"Are you *sure* you don't have any more food?" said Timonen.

The gnomes' vending machine had been turned upside down on the floor, which was littered with crumbs. Timonen had eaten it dry.

"I'm not answering that," said Grubchook.

He logged into the LEGENDS mainframe and ran a search.

"What are you looking for?" asked Saar.

"Magma Corps has to be registered somewhere," said

Grubchook. "We might have some data on them."

A graphic of an egg timer twisted and turned on the computer screen before settling. The screen blinked and a list of addresses rolled into view.

"Here's something," said Grubchook. "Magma Corporation, New York…"

"They're from America?" said Albrecht.

"Well, it's only their registered address," said Grubchook, "but it's a start."

"And what do they do?" asked Saar.

Grubchook scanned further through the files. "Makers of refrigeration devices and heating units."

"Yet they're out here in Antarctica studying volcanoes?" said Saar.

"Not only studying, but drilling into them," added Albrecht. "I smell a rat."

"I'd eat a rat right now," said Timonen.

"Would you shut up about food!" said Saar.

"So you can talk to me, but I can't answer back?" said Timonen.

"Stop this now," pleaded Albrecht.

"Well, if you'd only ask me what I thought about it all instead of leaving me out of your big important conversations…" said Timonen.

"All right, what *do* you think about it all?" asked Albrecht reluctantly.

"I think we should go to New York to find out for ourselves," he said. "I hear they do super-size meals out there. You gnomes could learn a thing or two."

"Ponkerton would never agree to it," said Albrecht. "There's too much risk of exposure."

"Does he need to know?" said Saar. "I've always fancied visiting the Big Apple."

"Hang on," said Albrecht, "aren't you normally the wise one?"

"I just sense that we already know something about Magma Corps," said Saar. "That masked man seemed familiar…"

"But New York is full of humans," said Albrecht. "We'd stick out like sore thumbs."

"You'd be surprised," said Grubchook. "I visited LEGENDS HQ in New York once. Big cities make blending in easy."

"No one noticed you because you're the size of a gnat," said Timonen. "It's more likely they'd tread on you."

"Timonen!" said Albrecht.

The gnome glared at Timonen.

"This oaf is your main worry," he said. "But if you can make him less stupid, you might just get away with it."

"That's impossible," said Saar.

"We should just tell Ponkerton," said Albrecht. "Let someone else deal with this."

"You're a scaredy-cat, too!" said Timonen.

"Am not," he said, biting his lip.

"Then call up Sherpa I," said Timonen. "Take me somewhere I can fill my stomach."

THE MYTHICAL **9th** DIVISION

Chapter 3: Undercover Yetis

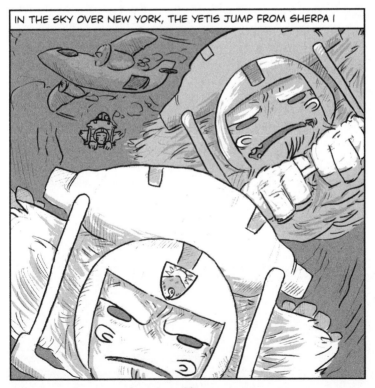

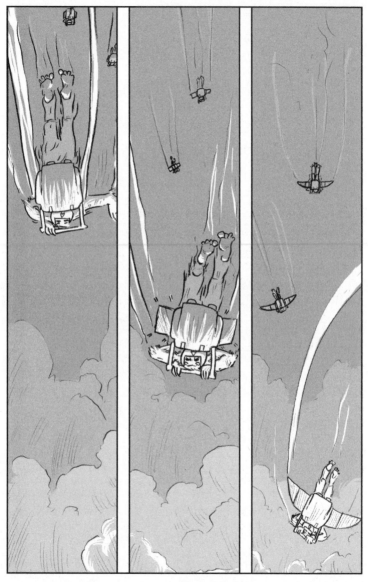

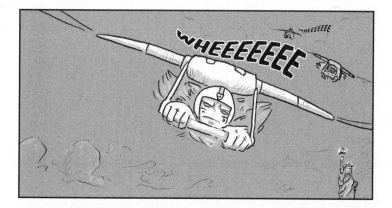

The hang gliders swooped between the skyscrapers of Manhattan, lit by the light escaping from offices and high-rise apartments.

"Follow me," said Albrecht through his comms system, tilting his hang glider downward.

He started his silent descent, struggling to keep the craft level as the wind bumped it sideways at every intersection. The grid system of roads made navigation easy, and although late-night pedestrians strolled up and down the streets, none bothered to look up. Albrecht's RoAR, clutched tightly in one hand, was displaying a 3-D map of the city, guiding him straight towards Central Park.

"The park should be empty at this hour," he said. "With a bit of luck, no one will notice us."

Saar's voice crackled through his earpiece.

"Don't forget this is the city that never sleeps," he said sagely.

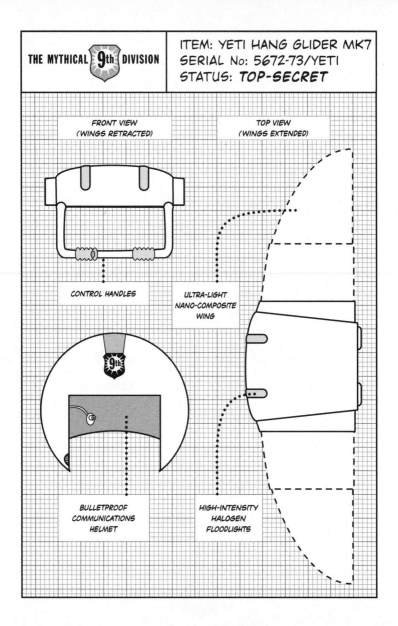

"We need to be ready for anything."

Timonen had good control of his hang glider, helped by his enormous weight.

"As long as there's food, I'm always ready," he said.

Skyscraper after skyscraper whizzed by, and the yetis were soon gliding close to the spidery traffic lights and bright-yellow taxis. Suddenly, with the onset of a strong gust of wind, the horizon opened out and the dark expanse of Central Park rushed into view.

Albrecht signaled for them to land. He pulled at his hand-grip as his feet skimmed the leaves of a thick band of trees. With an open piece of parkland in his sights he dropped to the ground for a gentle landing. The others bounced softly onto the beautifully mown lawn.

"So far so good," said Albrecht, removing his helmet.

He unlatched himself from his hang glider and closed its wings together. Once the other yetis had done the same, they ran across to the tree line.

"An easy landing," said Saar, placing his closed glider in a dense clump of bushes.

"And hopefully we evaded the radar," said Albrecht, placing his glider next to it.

"I can smell sausages," said Timonen, his eyes glazing over. "And fried onions!"

He threw his glider into the branches of a tree and hurried off in search of the source of the delicious smell.

"He's going to get us caught," said Saar.

"I've got him covered," said Albrecht calmly. "I don't feel half as worried now that we're here."

"I can't say the same," said Saar. "I can smell things other than food. There are strange four-legged creatures nearby. I'm beginning to wonder why I thought this was a good idea."

"There!" shouted Timonen, creating panic in Saar.

They'd reached the edge of the park and on the roadside was a street vendor selling hot dogs. Timonen's keen sense of smell had led him straight to it.

"If only he'd use his skills for something other than his stomach," said Saar.

The yetis kept out of sight behind a wall while Timonen formulated a plan. There were humans and traffic all around, but nothing was going to stop him.

"We need to create a diversion," said Timonen.

"This is going to end badly," said Albrecht. "Do you really need to eat now? You got through fifteen microwave pizzas on Sherpa I."

"That was just for starters," said Timonen. "You're not stopping me having a sausage."

Timonen read all the words on the vendor's cart. He'd never heard of half of what was for sale.

"Scratch that," he said. "I want a chili dog... No, I want a pretzel."

Albrecht clasped his head in his hands.

"What *is* a pretzel?" said Timonen.

"Just stick with the hot dog for now," said Saar.

"Maybe you're right," said Timonen, absolutely certain that coming to New York was the best thing he'd ever done. "Okay," he said impatiently. "Cover my back."

Before the others could stop him, Timonen leapt over the wall and ran towards the hot dog cart. A cluster of screams rang out from nearby pedestrians and Timonen dodged into

the road, causing a pileup between two taxis. Horns honked, drivers shouted, and with the cunning of a very hungry yeti, Timonen skirted around the edge of the stall and skillfully grabbed an armful of hot dogs.

"Hey! Stop that!" said the cart vendor, dropping a metal

spatula to the ground. He was more concerned about the theft than the fact that Timonen was the size of a house *and* a yeti.

"Tasty! Thanks," said Timonen, as he stuffed a hot dog in his mouth and hurried back to the wall. With a swift leap he was over and alongside his friends.

"What have you done?" said Saar, fuming.

"Scrum!" said Timonen, chewing and gulping at the same time.

"So the humans know we're here then?" said Albrecht. "This is a disaster."

A group of high-pitched sirens blasted out a few streets away.

"That's the sound of police cars," said Saar. "We're sitting ducks out here!"

"We need to find somewhere to hide," said Albrecht, his eyes scanning the park. He checked the map on the RoAR once more, moving its position with the touch of his fingers.

"I've got it," said Albrecht. "The subway! There's got to be somewhere to hide down there."

The yetis ran back into the park, skirting around the edge of a large pond and back under tree cover. The sirens were closing in and they had to stop abruptly when three police cars hurtled along a road that cut through the park. As searchlights criss-crossed the bushes and trees, the yetis dived to the ground.

"That was close," said Saar.

Albrecht caught his breath before carrying on.

"If we cut through here, we should be near an exit," he said.

"I could always just flatten the police," said Timonen, his growling stomach mildly comforted by the hot dogs.

"Do you honestly believe that's going to make things better?" said Saar.

"If you so much as touch a human," said Albrecht, "I promise you won't live to see another yak."

"All right, all right," said Timonen. "I'll do as you say… Just this once."

Once the police threat had gone, Albrecht dragged the others to their feet.

"Come on," he said tentatively. "The closest subway station is just a few streets away."

"This still sounds risky to me," said Saar.

"We don't have much choice," said Albrecht.

They crossed the road, crept back under tree cover and found a tall iron fence.

"If we follow this we can keep out of sight," said Albrecht, following the advice of his RoAR. "It'll lead us safely out of the park."

Timonen sniffed the air.

"I can smell polar bears," he said excitedly.

"That's because it's a zoo," said Albrecht. "Which is where they'll put you if you pull any more stupid stunts."

"But they might have yaks!" said Timonen, readying himself for the jump over the fence.

"Just think what you're about to do," grumbled Albrecht. "Now's not the time to stage a yak-rescue."

The look of happiness slipped from Timonen's face. He dragged his heels as he returned to Albrecht's side.

"You spoil everything," said Timonen.

"Someone has to," said Albrecht.

They paced through the undergrowth to edge of the park, where the brightly lit road looked far from welcoming.

"Are you sure this is a good idea?" said Saar. "I'm having serious second thoughts."

Suddenly an ear-piercing *whoop* screamed out from a car parked on the roadside. A powerful beam of light shot out from a light on its roof, and the yetis found themselves surrounded by four armed policemen.

"Get down on the ground!" ordered the nearest. "Hands where we can see them!"

"We're done for," said Albrecht.

"Shut up and get down on the ground!" shouted the policeman once more.

"Or else what?" growled Timonen, smashing his fist into his palm.

"They have guns," said Saar. "Take it easy, big boy."

"Do as he says," grumbled Albrecht, lowering himself to the ground. "Captain Ponkerton's going to skin us alive."

THE MYTHICAL **9th** DIVISION

Chapter 4: NYPD Fox

THE YETIS ARE SQUEEZED INTO A POLICE CAR

LET'S TAKE THEM DOWNTOWN FOR QUESTIONING.

59

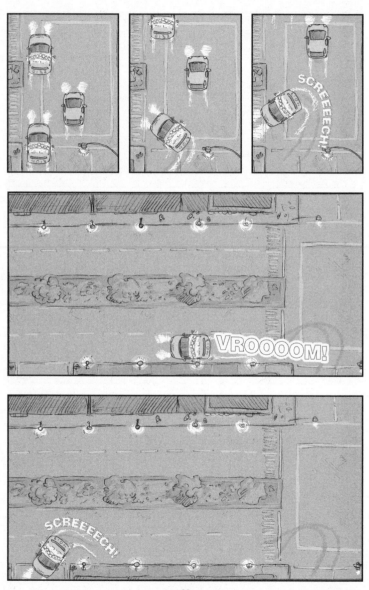

"**W**hy are we in a dead-end alley?" asked Albrecht.

The car slowed to a halt and the driver stepped out. They were surrounded by trash cans and the smell of rotting food.

"Okay," said the policeman. "Get out."

"He has a gun," said Saar. "I think we should stay here."

Timonen opened the door and stretched his cramped legs.

"I'm not staying in there with you," he said, sniffing the air. "Does that smell rotten or almost edible?"

"And the rest of you," said the policeman. "You don't have to worry."

Albrecht cautiously levered himself into the alley and Saar followed.

"Why have you brought us here?" asked Albrecht.

The policeman smiled.

"I smelled you as soon as you arrived in Central Park," he said.

"The big guy's stink is, well … stinky."

"I don't get you," said Albrecht.

The policeman passed him his police badge. Instead of saying NYPD, it held the emblem of the Mythical 8th Division.

"But that means…" said Albrecht.

"I'm Hiro," said the policeman, "leader of the kitsune division."

"You're a fox?" said Saar.

"I am," replied Hiro. "This is just a disguise."

"A fox?" said Timonen. "But where's your fur?"

"He's a shape-shifter," said Albrecht. "He can be any creature he likes."

"And it's lucky for you guys I make a good cop," said Hiro. "Now, one of you should explain why you're here."

"Food," said Timonen. "We came here because there is none in Antarctica."

"That's not strictly true," said Albrecht. "We're looking into

Magma Corps. Their offices are here."

"How come?" asked Hiro. "Your division shouldn't have been assigned an inner-city operation."

"Erm, we didn't really get assigned a mission," said Albrecht.

"So the people at LEGENDS don't know you're here?" said Hiro.

"You could say that," said Albrecht, feeling embarrassed.

"Then it's a good job I found you," he said. "I heard a radio alert about some freak in a Bigfoot costume stealing hot dogs. With that and your smell, I was pretty sure something odd was going on."

"I wish we'd stayed in Antarctica," said Saar.

"Sometimes you have to follow your instincts," said Hiro.

"One of us tends to follow them a little too much," said Saar, nodding at Timonen.

"My instincts are just fine," said Timonen.

"So where's this company based?" said Hiro.

"350 5th Avenue," said Albrecht.

Hiro snorted.

"You know what that is, right?" he said.

"No," said Albrecht, feeling foolish.

"It's the Empire State Building," said Hiro.

Albrecht looked to Saar for help.

"You know, King Kong…" he said.

"It's the most famous sight in New York," said Hiro. "And the most visited. Getting you in unnoticed won't be easy."

"We need a disguise," said Albrecht.

"That's not a bad idea," said Hiro. He sized up the yetis one by one. "I think I may have a solution."

"Sounds promising," said Saar.

"Yeah," said Hiro. "It might just work."

Hiro walked to his car and leaned inside to radio the police station. He lied beautifully about a problem with the engine then returned to the yetis.

"Right then," he said, rolling his shoulders. "We need to make a move. And you might want to turn away for a second."

Hiro's body blurred as it twisted and contorted and shrank down onto the ground. His clothes vanished and fur began to appear. In the blink of an eye he was a glorious kitsune once more. His nine tails swayed back and forth.

"Follow me," said Hiro. "We don't have much time before the sun rises."

"There are good ideas and there are bad ideas," said Saar. "And then there are utterly ludicrous ideas."

"So what's this one?" said Albrecht.

"Do I really need to answer?" said Saar.

It was morning, and the three yetis were walking down 5th Avenue in New York. The shops were busy, the streets even more so, but no one gave the yetis so much as a sideways look. This was solely due to the fact that they were wearing huge pink hippopotamus outfits and carrying signs advertising Hippo Fruit Chews: the biggest chews with the sweetest centers.

"I quite like it," said Timonen.

"You would," said Saar. "I feel like a traitor to my yeti ancestors and worst of all, I feel stupid."

"Timonen feels like that all the time," said Albrecht.

A quiet beep sounded in Albrecht's earpiece. Hiro's voice came through loud and clear.

"It's like Fort Knox in here," he said.

Hiro had gone ahead and was checking out the inside of the building.

"Have you found Magma Corps?" asked Albrecht.

"They're on the 75th floor," he replied. "And it's not going to be easy to reach them. There are guards, security passes … the works."

"So we may need more than pink hippo costumes?" said Albrecht.

"We'll see," said Hiro. "You should be almost there by now. I'll meet you outside."

After a brief stop to let Timonen tell a woman where she could buy some Hippo Fruit Chews – he was never one to let the truth get in the way of a search for food – the yetis reached the Empire State Building. It looked like any other skyscraper from the ground, but when the yetis looked up into the air its soaring stepped design revealed its majesty. It was far taller than any other building nearby, with its top finished off by an enormous spike.

"It's as tall as Everest," said Albrecht.

"1,250 feet exactly," said a bearded man in a suit. He stepped out onto the sidewalk and winked at Albrecht in his hippo costume.

"Hiro?" said Albrecht, noticing a small pin on his chest in the shape of a fox's tail.

"That's me," he replied. "You guys look awesome. I really like the polka-dot bows."

"As soon as I'm out of this costume," replied Saar, "I'm going to burn it."

"Well, you'll need it a little longer," said Hiro. "I reckon I can get you up to their offices, but you won't get past Magma Corps security."

"Leave that to me," said Timonen.

"You've got to realize that this is breaking every rule in the book," said Hiro. "You cannot be seen for what you really are."

"You should lock Timonen in a cell now then," said Saar. "This is very likely to go wrong."

"You've got to promise me you won't do anything stupid," said Hiro. "If LEGENDS find out I'm helping you, I'm dead meat. You guys aren't just risking your own necks up there."

"I promise," said Timonen. "You know me."

Saar groaned.

"Good," said Hiro. "Drop your signs and follow me."

The yetis and Hiro walked into the building through a set of ornate doors. The lobby shone with marble opulence, and high on the walls two American flags fluttered as a rush of air flooded past them. All three yetis were in awe of its size.

"We have nothing like this in Tibet," said Saar. "Not even the monasteries."

"This way," said Hiro, leading them to the information desk past a line of humans waiting to travel upstairs on the impressive elevators.

"Welcome to the Empire State Building!" said the attendant. "How can I help you?"

"I need to get these workers up to the 75th floor," said Hiro.

"Will they fit in the elevators in those outfits?" asked the attendant. "Otherwise the stairs are your best bet."

"Aren't there a lot of stairs?" asked Hiro.

"Over 1,800 to the top," she replied. "And you're going very near the top."

"Let's take the elevator," said Timonen.

"Elevator it is," said Hiro. "This way guys…"

When the elevator doors opened they were greeted by a man with a beard, who ushered them in and asked them for their floor number. Timonen stooped to fit inside, and even then his big hippo head was pressed firmly against the roof. A minute later the elevator pinged and the doors were opening again.

"Here we are," said Hiro.

The yetis stepped out onto the 75th floor and the elevator doors closed behind them.

Chapter 5: Beards and Fur

UMMM...

Hiro smiled and pushed the three pink hippos closer.

"I've brought these guys up for their interview," he said.

The man typed a few words into his computer.

"I'm sorry," he said, "but I have nothing on the calendar for this morning."

"Really?" said Hiro.

"I assure you," said Albrecht, speaking through his hippo head, "we have an interview with the manager. About advertising possibilities."

"There is nothing on the calendar," said the man. "I must ask you to leave. Have a nice day."

"Hmm," muttered Hiro.

He stepped back to play for time when suddenly the elevator doors pinged again. Three men with beards walked out carrying boxes. They swiped their passcards against a white box and walked through the doors into the office.

Albrecht pulled Hiro to one side and bent lower to whisper in his ear.

"We need one of those passcards," said Albrecht.

"Okay," said Hiro. "I'll leave you guys here while I go back to the lobby and see what I can do. At the first sniff of trouble, get out of here any way you can."

Hiro took the elevator and the yetis stood quietly, waiting for something to happen.

"Are you sure there's nothing on the calendar?" Saar asked the man at the desk. "We've come a very long way for this interview."

The man looked up from his computer screen.

"I have nothing on the calendar for this morning," he said. "Have a nice day."

"There's something funny about all these men with beards," said Timonen. "I don't trust a man with a beard."

"You realize that *you* have a beard," said Saar.

"But I'm a yeti," said Timonen.

"It's still a beard."

Albrecht sighed. "Look," he said to the man at the desk, "I

promise you, we have a meeting arranged."

The man was about to reply when a telephone rang on his desk. He picked it up, never letting his eyes leave the pink hippos.

"That was the manager," he said finally, placing the phone back on its receiver. "He's expecting you."

"Huh?" said Timonen. "But he can't be—"

"That's greatly appreciated," interrupted Albrecht.

The man pressed a button and the door beeped as it opened. "Please go through," he said.

The yetis looked at each other suspiciously through their hippo outfits, then walked inside.

They were surprised to find a normal, dreary office, with desks and tables, computers and workers, and two gigantic red "M"s painted on the far wall. There was nothing extraordinary about Magma Corps whatsoever.

"Do you think we've made a big mistake?" said Saar quietly.

"Who knows?" said Albrecht, looking around.

Timonen sniffed and stared at all the humans working quietly at computers.

"Do they really live like this?" he asked. "I'd be bored out of my brains."

"It's no existence for any creature," said Saar wisely.

Albrecht walked further into the office.

"Erm, excuse me," he said aloud. "We're here to see the manager."

The office workers looked up in unison from their computer screens.

"Beards…" whispered Timonen. "Beards everywhere…"

"The manager is in a meeting at present," said one of the men, pointing to a set of double doors on the far wall between the red "M"s. "Please take a seat and I'll let you know when he's available."

The worker directed the yetis to a row of chairs and they sat down.

"Why do you think he wants to see us?" said Albrecht, plumping up an M-shaped throw pillow.

"I don't know, but I think we should be on our guard," said Saar. "There's a very odd atmosphere about this place."

"Everyone looks brain dead," said Timonen. "Although

you'd have to be to work in a place like this."

A telephone rang on the worker's desk, and after a short conversation, the yetis became the focus of his attention.

"The manager will see you now," he said, walking over to them. "Please come with me to the boardroom."

The yetis hauled themselves up and followed him towards the double doors on the far wall, which opened automatically for the visitors.

The walls of the boardroom were covered in giant framed posters of refrigerators and air-conditioning systems – staple products of the Magma Corporation range. A huge black table sat in the center of the room, and at its furthest point was a high-backed leather chair facing the wall. The manager was sitting waiting for them.

"So we meet again," he said evilly, spinning the chair around so that he could see the pink hippos. It was none other than the man they'd seen in Antarctica! But this time his black welder's mask was flicked back on top of his head. Albrecht recognized his face immediately.

"Balaclava!" he gasped. "But I saw you fall to your death…"

Timonen furrowed his brow.

"Who's Balaclava?" he said.

"For goodness' sake…" said Saar. "Remember Wales? Last summer? Mini ice age? Turned your fur white?"

"Oh," said Timonen. "Him!"

"Of course!" said Balaclava. "And I take it that under those ridiculous outfits I'll find three annoying yetis?"

Albrecht looked at his friends and removed his suit. Timonen and Saar did the same. There was no point in pretending anymore.

Balaclava laughed. "I've been itching to get my own back at you ever since you destroyed my mountain base."

"Want me to pummel him?" said Timonen.

"Only after he's told us what he was doing in Antarctica," said Albrecht, "and what he's up to in New York."

"Oh, I wouldn't be quite so hasty," said Balaclava, flicking a switch on the arm of his chair.

A door opened in the wall of the boardroom and a huge white robot marched out. It stopped behind Balaclava, dwarfing him completely. Steam spurted from its joints as it settled.

"Yetis, meet my new super robot," said Balaclava. "The Greebo X."

"It's even bigger than Timonen," said Albrecht.

"I could still smash it to pieces, though," said Timonen.

"I wouldn't upset a Greebo X," said Balaclava, rubbing his gloved hands together.

The robot's eyes lit up and a panel slid backwards on its forearm to reveal a flamethrower. A tiny flame fluttered at its end.

"Ooh, scary," said Timonen.

A jet of fire shot from the weapon, hitting the ground just in front of the big yeti's feet.

"Hey, watch my toenails!" said Timonen. "I need them for snacks."

"So," said Balaclava, rising from his chair. "You're in a very difficult position. You really never should have come here."

"We've beaten you once and we can do it again," said Albrecht. "You're still outnumbered."

"Outnumbered?" said Balaclava. "Look behind you!"

The yetis turned to look through the office doors where the

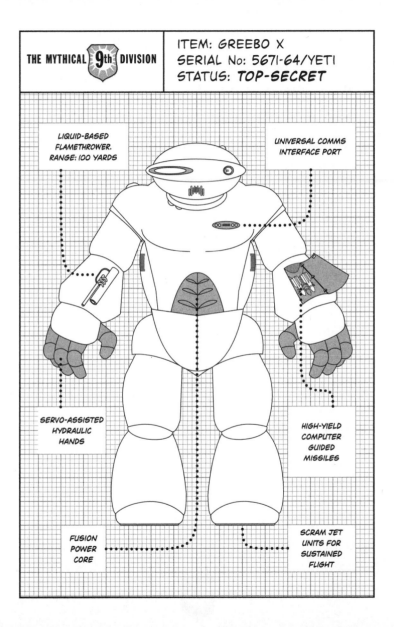

workers were staring at them. Their eyes glowed red and their beards fizzed with static.

"What's wrong with them?" said Saar.

"Nothing," said Balaclava. "They're my newly humanized Greebo 1000s. I call them Greeboids."

"They're robots?" said Albrecht.

"The beards!" said Timonen. "I knew it. Never trust a beard."

"The Greeboids require beards to hide a visible join in the fake skin," said Balaclava. "I hope to remove the need for them by the next model."

"Flaming yaks, they could be anywhere," said Saar, realizing what this revelation meant. "People have beards the world over."

"But of course!" said Balaclava. "How else could I have set up my latest plan for world domination?"

"What are you up to?" snarled Albrecht.

Balaclava pressed another button on the arm of his chair and the wall posters transformed into digital displays. A section of the black table slid sideways, revealing a computer, and Balaclava typed in some commands. Images of an erupting volcano filled the screens.

"Remember this?" he said, enjoying the moment. "A searing blast of pure fire and brimstone!"

"That's Mount Erebus," said Albrecht.

"My Antarctic test run," said Balaclava.

"*You* set off the volcano?" said Saar.

"With the touch of a button," Balaclava gloated.

The screens flickered to another image of a volcano, this time situated behind a city.

"This is Vesuvius," said Balaclava. "And in the corner of the picture you might see one of my drill tanks. It delivered its payload just a few minutes ago."

"Payload?" said Saar.

"A small device I've named the Volcanized Eruptor," said Balaclava, "capable of triggering a massive increase in pressure within the heart of a volcano's magma chamber."

The displays switched pictures once more. Another volcano, another drill tank.

"Mount Etna," said Balaclava, watching as the image changed again. "And Mount Galeras... You get the gist."

"You have no idea what you're doing," said Saar. "You're playing with fire!"

"That's what I love about it," said Balaclava.

"You're crazy," said Albrecht.

"Nope," replied Balaclava, "just good at spotting a niche in the world-domination market."

"But nature is wild," said Saar. "You can't hope to control volcanoes."

"I don't need to control them," said Balaclava. "I just need to make them erupt. I will demand a ransom for each volcano that I've primed – the greater the potential damage, the greater the cost."

"What if the world won't pay?" said Albrecht.

"Ah," he replied. "But the world *will* pay. I have devised a top-secret weapon to ensure it."

"What is it?" said Albrecht."

"It's top-secret," said Balaclava. "I may be an evil genius and I may revel in revealing my plans, but even I draw the line at that. In any case, now that my cover is blown, I might as well get this show on the road!"

Balaclava unveiled a hidden panel in his black table.

"See this big red button marked DOOM?" said Balaclava. "When I press it, a volcano of my choice will erupt."

"You can't do that!" said Albrecht.

"Hmm," said Balaclava obliviously, pacing back and forth. "But which volcano shall I choose?"

The evil genius navigated through a list of volcanoes on his computer and settled on Vesuvius.

"Perfect!" he said. "A huge amount of damage can be done with this one. My first explosion should really make a statement."

"You're totally insane," said Albrecht.

"Not insane," said Balaclava, "evil. And now let me contact the United Nations."

He picked up the phone and hit a single digit.

"The sign of a true evil genius," said Balaclava, "is having the brains to put the United Nations Global Threat Department on speed dial."

The phone rang three times before the answering machine kicked in.

"You have reached the hotline of the United Nations Global

Threat Department," said the voice. "If your query is urgent, please leave a message after the beep and we'll get back to you as soon as we can. *BEEP!*"

Balaclava was slightly flustered.

"Urgent!" he said. "Of course this is urgent! I am the evil genius Balaclava and if you do not transfer one billion dollars into my bank account within the next five minutes, I will use my latest invention to create a massive volcanic eruption at Mount Vesuvius. Thousands of humans will lose their lives if you do not agree to my terms. And this is just the beginning. An account number for the transferal of funds is heading to you now."

Balaclava huffed before finishing.

"I look forward to hearing from you."

He replaced the receiver and turned to the yetis.

"You see how easy it is?" he said. "Five minutes to payment, or eruption."

"Five minutes if they get back to you," said Albrecht.

He leapt forward, attempting to grab Balaclava, but the Greebo X stamped to attention and knocked him back.

"Silly yeti," laughed Balaclava.

He paced back and forth for three minutes before checking his online bank account. There were no new funds.

"They haven't paid me!" he exclaimed, looking to his Greebo X furiously. The robot's metal features didn't allow it a response. Balaclava picked up the phone once more and pressed redial. He got the answering machine message once more and waited for the beep.

"You've got two minutes left," he said. "Where's my money?"

There was a click, and a voice broke through onto the line.

"Hello, sir," said a lady. "We looked into your last threat and we have reason to believe you're a prank caller. Our records show that the real Balaclava is dead."

"What do you mean, I'm dead?" he said, laughing wildly. "You don't believe me?"

"Please calm down, sir," said the lady.

"Calm down?!" exclaimed Balaclava. "You've just told me I'm dead! When Mount Vesuvius blows up you'll wish you'd done your research!"

He slammed the phone down and his maniacal laughter grew louder and louder.

"They don't believe me!" he cried. "THEY DON'T BELIEVE ME!"

His thick glove moved closer to the DOOM button.

"This will make them believe me—"

He was cut short by the sound of the fire alarm wailing through the office.

"WHAT!?" said Balaclava. "I disengaged the fire alarms!"

A Greeboid entered Balaclava's office.

"We're having a fire drill," it said, its red eyes returning to normal momentarily.

"WE CAN'T HAVE A FIRE DRILL WHEN I'M ABOUT TO BLOW UP A VOLCANO!" Balaclava stomped in fury.

"The Fire Department is on its way," said the Greeboid.

"They can't come here. THEY CAN'T COME HERE!"

The main office doors opened and a bearded fire attendant appeared. He was dressed in a bright-yellow coat and held a clipboard in his hand. He looked at the office workers clumped around the boardroom like a crowd of zombies.

"Why are you not leaving the premises?" he said, looking a

little puzzled. "You should all be evacuating the building!"

Balaclava was left with no choice. "Get him!" he screamed.

The Greeboids turned en masse to face the fire attendant, their arms stretched out like zombies. But they were too late. With a blur of fur and in the blink of an eye, the fire attendant morphed into a glorious orange kitsune. His nine tails swirled like a cyclone, helping him skip nimbly across the floor for cover.

"Sorry, Albrecht – the fire alarm was my last hope!"

"It's Hiro!" shouted Albrecht. "Now's our chance."

"What?!" snapped Balaclava. "What was that?"

The yetis rolled under the table just as the Greebo X unleashed a jet of flame that sliced the boardroom in two.

"NO! NO! NO!" screamed Balaclava.

"Saar, go help Hiro with those Greeboids," said Albrecht. "Leave Balaclava to me. Timonen, you get the big robot."

"COME ON!" roared Timonen and scrambled into the open.

"Destroy the yetis!" cried Balaclava.

As Saar made a move for the door, Timonen leapt at the

giant robot's chest and clambered around onto its back.

"Go, Timonen!" shouted Albrecht, charging around the table and throwing himself at Balaclava, pinning the evil genius to the floor by his gloved hands.

"You're finished!" he said triumphantly.

Saar slipped out into the office, dodging squares of burning carpet. He vaulted a desk and caught the low-hanging blocks of strip lighting. He swung from one to another, and with a final dramatic leap, landed at Hiro's side.

"Who on earth *are* these bearded guys?" said the fox, weaving in and out of a Greeboid's legs.

Saar flicked his scarf over his shoulder and thrust his staff into the Greeboid's stomach, sending it sprawling on the ground. With a spark of electricity and a plume of smoke, its head split in two. Wires tumbled out like entrails.

"Robots," said Saar plainly. He spun around and decapitated another Greeboid with his staff.

"That would explain it," said Hiro.

• • •

Back in the boardroom, Timonen smashed his fists into the Greebo X with all his might.

"It's hard as nails!" growled Timonen, dodging jets of fire from the robot's flamethrower. His fingers were getting more and more numb with each punch and the Greebo X was growing angrier by the second. It jerked and convulsed, and to Albrecht, still pinning Balaclava to the floor, it looked as if Timonen was riding a bucking bronco.

"You're ruining everything!" cried Balaclava.

The boardroom was filling with smoke and the walls had caught fire. Sprinklers burst into action and rained down like a spring shower, catching Albrecht unaware.

Sensing weakness, the evil genius knocked Albrecht sideways and made for the other side of the table.

"That's the last time you touch me, yeti," said Balaclava, rising to his feet. He clunked the welder's mask down over his face. "My supersuit is far better equipped now..."

With a burst of steam a section of his gloved right hand flipped down to reveal a weapon. A tiny flame fluttered at its end.

"Shake hands?"

A searing bolt of fire spat from his glove, and Albrecht just managed to dodge it. The computer terminals burst into flames, and Albrecht rolled away to safety. Balaclava realized his mistake: the DOOM button had melted into an unworkable lump.

"I hate you hairy nuisances!" he shouted at Albrecht. "You'll pay for this."

"Do your worst," said Albrecht. "The world's safe now."

"Never!" said Balaclava. "The DOOM button was the gentle option. You leave me no choice but to initiate Ultimate Doom."

With his fire hand trained on Albrecht to stop him coming any closer, he opened a hidden drawer in the side of the table. A metal console slid out, bearing an even larger button: ULTIMATE DOOM. With the full force of his fist, he hammered it down.

The lights in the room flashed and a robotic voice boomed through the office.

"ULTIMATE DOOM INITIATED."

Balaclava laughed and turned on Albrecht.

"Now, my yeti," he said, the flame flickering in his palm, "it's time to burn."

THE MYTHICAL 9th DIVISION

Chapter 6: Ultimate Doom

BALACLAVA'S HAND TREMBLES AS HE CONTOLS THE FIREBALL

CHOKKA CHOKKA

CHOKKA CHOKKA

CHOKKA CHOKKA

96

IT'S THE MYTHICAL 6TH! WE'RE SAVED.

Saar and Hiro were barricaded behind three fallen desks, protecting their fragile defenses, when the Bigfoot troops stormed the office. As they knocked out the legion of Greeboids with beams of pinpoint laser fire, Balaclava sensed time was running out and called upon his Greebo X for help.

"Initiate escape sequence: Empire State," he said.

The giant robot's upper half began to spin like a whirlwind, sending Timonen flying into the wall and knocking him out. The robot kicked the table into Albrecht's path, then knelt down ready for its master.

"Get me out of here," said Balaclava, clambering up onto its back.

He tugged a handle at the base of the Greebo's neck and

metal fingers extended from its waist to create a seat. Balaclava leaned back and fastened the harness. "Let's go!" he ordered.

The Greebo X stomped into the office, swiping Bigfoot troops out of its path as it headed towards a window.

"Stop him!" shouted Albrecht. "He's going to escape."

But as their well-placed laser fire ricocheted off the robot's armor, the Bigfoot troops realized they were powerless. With its enormous fist clenched tight, the Greebo X punched through a window and clawed away part of the brick wall.

"Engage rockets," said Balaclava.

A belch of hot air spat from two vents on the robot's back and with a mighty roar the Greebo jetted off into the cold New York air.

Balaclava had escaped.

Buck, the leader of the Bigfoot regiment, marched around the devastated office, corralling any remaining Greeboids into a corner. The sprinklers were still in full flow and "ULTIMATE DOOM INITIATED" boomed repeatedly over the PA system.

"Where are you?" shouted Buck, sliding his goggles back onto his head. "Where's that yeti?"

Saar raised his hands into the air, signaling to Bigfoot troops that he was there and not an enemy.

"Not you!" shouted Buck. "Where's the yeti with the backpack?"

Timonen stumbled dizzily out of the boardroom and tripped over a malfunctioning Greeboid, flying straight into the arms of a Bigfoot. Albrecht crept out after him.

"You!" barked Buck. "What have you gone and done?"

Albrecht was resigned.

"It wasn't supposed to turn out like this," he said, sighing.

"ULTIMATE DOOM INITIATED," boomed the PA system.

"And what is that?" barked Buck.

"Yeah," said Albrecht meekly. "We need to look into that…"

"Too right we do," growled Buck. "This is the second time we've had to come and finish off what you guys started. Can't you do anything right?"

Hiro appeared from behind the desks, slipping gracefully through Greeboid carcasses.

"I'll check the computer system," he said, morphing back into the fire attendant's form. "We might be able to gather some information."

"Good idea," said Albrecht keenly, moving in to help.

"Don't even think about it," said Buck, thrusting his index finger in Albrecht's direction. "This is the most disastrous situation in LEGENDS history. The whole of New York is out there watching."

"It is?" said Albrecht.

Buck gripped the strap of Albrecht's backpack and dragged him to the open window. The view of New York stretched for miles, but when Albrecht looked down at the streets below, all he could see were swarming crowds of people pointing up at the building.

"Ah," he said.

"You're gonna have a hard time explaining this one," said Buck.

The Empire State Building had been fully evacuated by the time the yetis and Bigfoot troops climbed up to the observatory on the top floor. A Bigfoot regimental helicopter hovered overhead, with safety harnesses ready to pull the troops up.

"Get on!" ordered Buck.

"All right," said Albrecht. "We're not idiots."

"You'll have a hard time convincing Commander Millicent of that," said Buck.

The yetis were winched to safety, and as they took their seats, Buck joined them.

"Where are you taking us?" asked Saar.

"LEGENDS HQ," said Buck. "The noises I'm hearing down the line say you're gonna be debriefed to within an inch of your lives."

"We don't wear briefs," said Timonen. "Only girly Bigfoot soldiers wear briefs."

"You're gonna wish you never said that," said Buck.

The helicopter powered off across Manhattan. It flew along the Hudson River, dipping and turning slightly before landing among the United Nations buildings. LEGENDS HQ was housed in a subterranean level of the main complex. It had no floor number and could only be reached by a secret elevator.

As well as being the control center of the mythical divisions, it was also the center of Bigfoot operations, so Buck was very much at home.

After a short walk through the secret tunnels, the yetis were marched into a formal meeting room. Commander Millicent was sitting at a desk with a furious expression on her face, and on a huge video wall, Captain Ponkerton stared out at them. Albrecht had never seen him look so angry.

"I should court-martial you right now!" said Captain

Ponkerton. "What ever possessed you to go to a place like New York?!"

"We thought it was the right thing to do, sir," said Albrecht.

"Why didn't you consult me first?" he replied. "As you now know, we already had operatives in the city."

"Yes, sir," said Albrecht, looking at his toes, "but this was our mission – or it felt like it should be…"

"What you felt is not important," Ponkerton exploded. "You should be ashamed of yourselves. Especially you, Saar. I thought you'd have more sense!"

"I don't know what came over me," said Saar, turning pink around the ears.

"I hope you realize you've jeopardized the whole future of LEGENDS?" said Ponkerton. "We now have the world's media on our heels and photos of Balaclava are circulating on the web."

"That part could have been handled better," admitted Albrecht. "But we did travel in disguise—"

"Disguise?" argued Commander Millicent. "You were dressed as pink hippos!"

"That was Hiro's idea," said Timonen.

"And he won't be coming out of this unscathed, either," said Millicent. "At least he had the sense to call us when he lost contact with you."

The meeting room doors slammed open and Buck marched into the room, looking like a true hero with his glossy brown fur swept back over his head. He swaggered across to Commander Millicent.

"I've received word of major volcanic eruptions around the globe," he said seriously. "It appears they started simultaneously."

"Where?" asked Albrecht.

"All major continents," said Buck.

"Get me visuals," said Millicent, snapping into action.

"They should be streaming already," he said. "Channel 9 on your video wall."

The screen of Ponkerton's face gravitated to one side as a live news feed filled the rest of the video wall. The bright-red glow of scorching-hot lava shone into the room.

———— 9th ————

THE MYTHICAL 9th DIVISION

Chapter 7: LEGENDS HQ

VOLCANOES AROUND THE WORLD ERUPT IN VIOLENT DISPLAYS OF POWER

MT VESUVIUS, ITALY

MT POPOCATEPETL, MEXICO

MT FUJI, JAPAN

MT GALERAS, COLOMBIA

Albrecht was holding his head in his hands.

"This was our fault," he said gravely.

"Is this the end of it?" asked Ponkerton.

Albrecht shook his head.

"Balaclava had loads of volcanoes lined up," he said.

"Then we need to mobilize land troops," said Millicent, "and lots of them. We've got to start evacuating people living near any potential volcanic threat."

"He also talked about a secret back-up plan to ensure he gets his money," said Saar.

"Balaclava is after payback for what happened in Snowdonia," explained Albrecht. "He was after a billion dollar ransom, and if that wasn't paid we should assume the secret plan has been put into action."

"Then we need to find out what it is," said Ponkerton. "We also need to pinpoint Balaclava's position."

"Hiro was checking the computer systems at Magma Corps," said Albrecht. "Have we heard anything from him?"

"Last time I saw him, he was in the decryption room," said Buck.

"Then find him," said Commander Millicent. "If we have any luck, we might yet get a chance to sort out this mess."

"Yetis," said Ponkerton. "Though you've broken every rule in the LEGENDS handbook, you did uncover something sinister. For that we should be grateful."

Commander Millicent nodded.

"Don't think there won't be punishment," said Millicent, "but you should get some rest now. We'll need you in tiptop condition for the next battle."

Millicent checked a list on her desk.

"Buck," she said, "get them some food. Show them some Bigfoot hospitality."

"Yes, ma'am," said Buck.

"And try to teach them a thing or two about following orders while you're at it," said Millicent.

Buck saluted.

"So," said Ponkerton, "until we hear more, over and out!"

The screen fizzled to black and Commander Millicent picked up the phone and asked for the head of the Mythical 2nd Division. She looked at Buck and gestured for him to take the yetis.

"I'll be in touch as soon as we have new information," she said. "In the meantime, make sure they don't do anything else stupid."

"Right then, guys," said Buck, as soon as they were outside, "what say I treat you to dinner Bigfoot-style?"

"Food?" exclaimed Timonen, bouncing on the spot with excitement.

"Sounds great," said a crestfallen Albrecht.

"Then follow me."

He led the yetis through a maze of brightly lit corridors until they reached a set of white doors draped with American flags.

"Welcome to a little slice of home," he said.

The doors swung wide and they were hit with the over-whelming smell of fried onions. The room was an all-American diner, brightly colored in red and blue, with chrome tables, high

...nd photos of the Bigfoot division covering the walls. At
...ter stood a Bigfoot, dressed in a chef's outfit.

"Yo, Buck!" he said, lifting his hand in the air. "You found
yourself some yetis!"

"These guys are the Mythical 9th Division," said Buck. "Put
on four of your best rib-eye steaks. And lots of fries."

"Erm … excuse me," said Saar, trying not to be rude. "I
don't suppose you have any tofu instead of steak?"

TODAY'S
SPECIAL

STEAK
AND
FRIES!

"What's tofu?" said Buck.

"It's what you eat instead of meat," said Saar.

"You eat stuff instead of meat? That sounds weird."

"I have no idea what Saar's problem is," said Timonen, drooling helplessly.

"People do eat things *other* than meat," said Saar. "I'm a vegetarian."

"Riiight," said Buck, understanding at last. "Sit over there and I'll see what else we have."

The yetis sat down as Buck leaned across the counter to whisper to the Bigfoot chef, who scratched his head.

"Nope, we've just got steak and fries," said the chef loudly. "That's it. No one's asked for anything else before."

"Looks like it's fries then," said Buck, returning to the yetis. "Sorry about that. Us Bigfoot don't eat much else."

"I'll survive," said Saar calmly. "I'm quite partial to chips."

"Chips?" asked Buck, "I might be able to get those for you."

"No," said Saar, realizing the confusion, "I meant fries. These things always muddle me. Biscuits and cookies, pants and trousers, you know…"

"Ah," said Buck. "I get you. I forget about your strange names for things."

"Well," said Saar. "I wouldn't say we're the strange ones…"

"Everyone's different," said Albrecht diplomatically.

"Here you go, guys!" said the Bigfoot chef. He was carrying four massive plates which he laid on the table.

Timonen couldn't hold back. He grabbed the steak and bit into it with abandon, the bloody juices running down his chin.

"Lovely," said Saar sarcastically, diverting his attention to the mound of fries in front of him.

"This is the best steak ever," said Timonen, licking his lips.

"We aim to please," said Buck proudly.

"So how does a notorious criminal like Balaclava manage to set up a base in a skyscraper unnoticed," asked Saar, trying not to look at Timonen.

"Good question," said Buck. He dipped a fry into some mustard and sucked it dry. "That's something we'll have to look into, although it was you guys who gave us the intel that he'd fallen to his death."

Luckily, Albrecht's RoAR chose that moment to start

beeping. He put down his knife and fork and removed the device from his backpack.

"Good afternoon," said the RoAR. "There is a video call waiting. Press the talk button to ... er ... talk."

Albrecht pressed the button.

"Hello?" he said.

"Evening," said Grubchook, his picture flashing up on the RoAR's screen. "I wondered whether I'd get you."

"I'm glad you did," said Albrecht. "What's up?"

"Magma Corps," he said. "We've got some more information."

"I don't know if you've heard," said Albrecht, "but we found them already – it didn't go well."

"I saw that on the mainframe," said Grubchook. "I've been following it closely, working on the volcanic data we've been getting from all these eruptions."

"Hey, gnome!" said Timonen, grabbing the RoAR. "This is what a real meal looks like. See?"

He directed the RoAR's camera to his plate, but Albrecht grabbed it back as fast as it was taken.

"Sorry about him," said Albrecht. "Carry on."

"There's a pattern emerging," said Grubchook. "We've gone through our global records and found a small increase in emissions from each of the target volcanoes prior to the new eruption."

"Possibly from his drilling?" said Saar.

"Could be," said Grubchook.

"Brilliant," said Albrecht. "So you can find his other targets by searching for similar emissions?"

"Already done it," said Grubchook. "I've forwarded the positions to LEGENDS."

"Good work," said Albrecht.

His RoAR beeped and a call-waiting symbol appeared. He said goodbye to Grubchook and answered. It was Commander Millicent.

"I take it Grubchook's filled you in on our current situation?" she said.

"Yes—"

"Then finish your food and get back up here," she said. "Hiro's found something."

Buck shot up from his seat and tore a final chunk out of his steak.

"You guys ready?" he said, flicking fur from his eyes.

Timonen stood up and burped.

"Let's go smash some robots," he said.

Back in the LEGENDS meeting room, Commander Millicent was wading through the mission details with Captain Winston Everhard, the human representative of the Mythical 6th Division. Captain Ponkerton was present via the video wall and Hiro was sitting on the floor in his natural form. His tails were curled around his body, their ends gently flitting up and down.

With two loud knocks, the meeting room door opened and Buck and Albrecht entered.

"You're ready for us?" said Buck.

"Too right," said Captain Everhard, striding over and slapping his troop on the back.

"We need you to prepare for battle," said Ponkerton, focusing on Albrecht.

Commander Millicent got down to business.

"Hiro uncovered Balaclava's bank details and business

dealings," she said. "He's been funding a new construction in the heart of Yellowstone National Park."

"Where's that?" asked Albrecht.

"The Northwest," said Buck. "In the Rocky Mountains."

"More importantly," said Millicent, "the park is situated in the crater of a super volcano."

"A super volcano?" said Albrecht.

"A volcano so large," said Ponkerton, "that if it erupted, it would wipe out half of America."

"It's that huge?" said Albrecht.

"And its emissions would play havoc with Earth's atmosphere," said Millicent. "We'd be thrown into a new ice age. Crops wouldn't grow, people would die of hunger—"

"Then we need to act immediately!" said Albrecht.

Captain Everhard spread huge rolls of satellite imagery from Yellowstone National Park across Millicent's desk.

"We don't have much to go on," he said, "but these man-made structures should be the focus of our attention."

Everhard pointed to a number of unusual buildings across the map. "These weren't there a month ago. They've been put up in secret. I've contacted some friends in the area and no Park Ranger knows they exist."

"All we know is they're situated on key thermal hot spots," said Millicent.

"Are they drill sites?" said Albrecht.

"You'll need to find that out," said Ponkerton.

"Then take us there now!" said Albrecht.

"Oh, don't worry, we're sending you in all right," said Commander Millicent. "But you're on Bigfoot territory here. I want Captain Everhard to call the shots."

"What?" said Albrecht angrily. "This is our mission."

"Not anymore," said Ponkerton.

"In my view," said Everhard, "the yetis are surplus to requirements."

"That's a rather short-sighted opinion," said Ponkerton.

"I'm with Ponkerton," said Commander Millicent. "Yellowstone is suffering its worst winter in years. You need their experience."

"My troops have all the gear needed to deal with subzero missions," said Captain Everhard. "We don't need yeti help."

"I believe you do," said Millicent forcefully. "Albrecht has dealt with Balaclava before. Your teams are stronger together."

"I can't be responsible for their safety," said Buck.

"I can't be responsible for *your* safety," replied Albrecht.

"Ha!" laughed Captain Everhard. "My Buck is the best there is."

"Your Buck?" began Captain Ponkerton. "My Albrecht—"

"That's enough," said Millicent, her attention on a beep from her pager. "The helicopters are ready," she said. "It's time."

Buck held out his hand for Albrecht to shake.

"If I'm stuck with you, let's make the best of it," he said. "Let's go save the world!"

Albrecht shook his hand and turned to Ponkerton. He knew he had a lot to prove.

"Balaclava won't get away this time," he promised.

Balaclava's secret base was an underground lair, deep in the bedrock of Yellowstone National Park. Constructed of heat-proof metal, with minimal access to the outside world, Balaclava had learned his lesson from his previous base in Wales: it would be very difficult for anyone to see it.

A laboratory to all things red and hot, Balaclava's new mission control had given birth to many fruit. Tapping into the veins of lava that traveled out of Earth's core, the evil genius had harnessed an unlimited supply of power, and in the process, fashioned a hardened metal impervious to heat. Initially Balaclava used his new material for his drill tanks, but it was soon clear that the impenetrable metal had other uses, not least the Greebo X armor and Balaclava's bright-red supersuit.

With his supersuit and mask, Balaclava was protected from the sulfur and noxious fumes emitted from the thermal vents, and he proudly strutted around his base.

"I'll have to blow up Yellowstone soon," proclaimed Balaclava restlessly. "It won't be long before they find me."

He stepped across an open stream of lava, which crossed the room like a steaming bright-red ribbon.

"Greebo X warriors in position," said a Greeboid, dressed in lumberjack gear with a yellow hard hat. Its red beard traveled all the way to its belt.

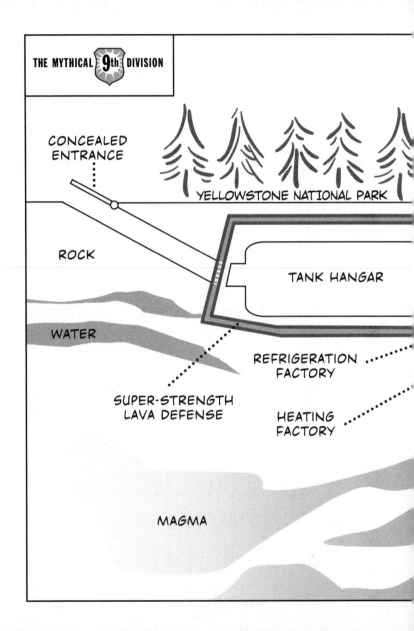

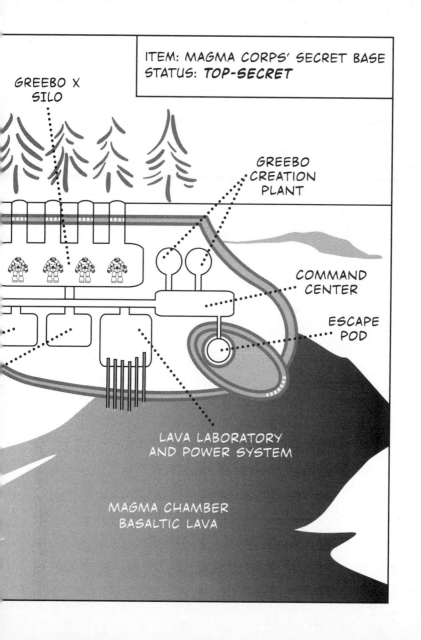

"Good," said Balaclava. "And how long until the initial Volcanized Eruptors are in place?"

"Three drill tanks are moving into position," said the robot. "The extreme weather is slowing us down."

"Well, get them to hurry up," said Balaclava. "The crust needs to be weakened for the Magma Bomb to have the maximum effect!" He turned around to focus on a huge metallic cylinder held aloft on the back of his drill tank. It was a super-sized version of a Volcanized Eruptor.

"Is this ready for priming?" he asked, surveying the device.

"Yes," said the robot. "The volcanic rods require four hours to engage."

"Then everything is taking shape," said Balaclava. "Those yetis will be sorry they meddled."

He walked over to the huge Greebo X that helped him escape from New York and clambered up onto the control seat.

"The furry fiends won't know what's hit them."

THE MYTHICAL 9th DIVISION

Chapter 8: Yellowstone

THE BIGFOOT HELICOPTERS REACH YELLOWSTONE NATIONAL PARK

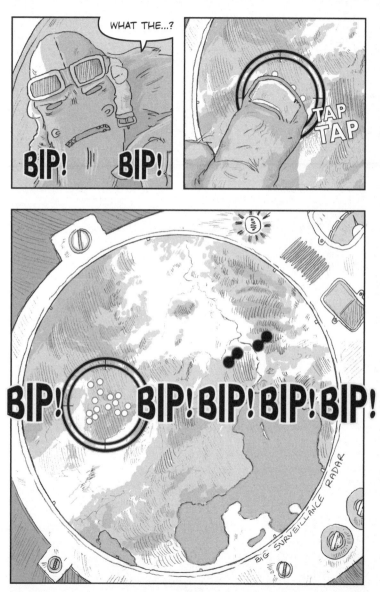

129

"**C**hopper 1, this is Chopper 2," crackled the radio inside the yetis' helicopter. "Take evasive action. Bogies incoming."

"Flying snot?" said Timonen, tugging at his safety buckle. "Let me see!"

"Stay there!" ordered Buck, unlocking his own safety belt.

The Bigfoot rushed to the front-mounted laser cannon and surveyed the area, sweeping the laser from left to right.

"Got 'em," he said, growling.

"What are they?" said Albrecht.

"Huge flying robots," said Buck. He dropped the safety catch and the laser cannon powered up.

"Sounds like Greebo Xs," said Albrecht. He tried to remain calm, but in the air the yetis were next to useless. "You've got to get us on the ground before they strike."

Buck fired his lasers through the air, but the chances of hitting anything were minimal. The robots closed in.

Saar looked out through the circular window behind him. "There are at least twelve of them," he said. "And hey – weren't they laser-proof?"

"Here they come!" shouted Buck, ignoring Saar. "Hold tight!"

A fireball hit the helicopter's hull and flame rippled over its side. Three Greebo Xs shot up past them and turned cartwheels in the sky.

"Take us down!" barked Albrecht. "We'll stand a chance on the ground."

"These choppers can take fireballs," said Buck confidently. He fired the laser once again, its jagged beams curving past their attackers.

The second helicopter buzzed alongside, smoke pouring from its rear engine. A Greebo X was attached to its side, stripping away metal panels from the engine.

"They're in trouble!" said Buck. "We need to do something."

Albrecht was desperate. He unclasped his safety belt and marched over to Buck.

"Land it," he said, gripping the Bigfoot by the arms.

Buck lost his temper.

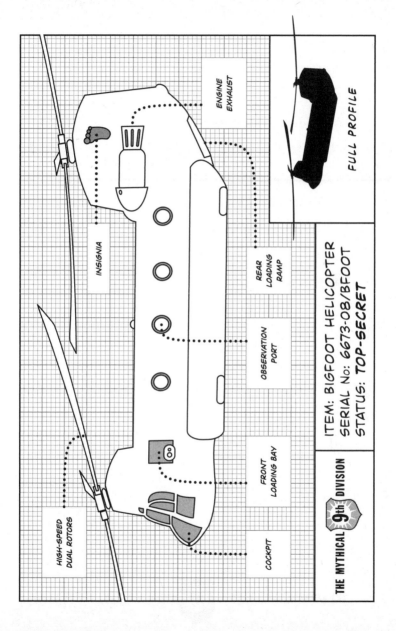

ENGINE EXHAUST

FULL PROFILE

INSIGNIA

REAR LOADING RAMP

OBSERVATION PORT

FRONT LOADING BAY

HIGH-SPEED DUAL ROTORS

COCKPIT

ITEM: BIGFOOT HELICOPTER
SERIAL No: 6673-08/BFOOT
STATUS: *TOP-SECRET*

THE MYTHICAL **9**th DIVISION

"Restrain him!" he ordered.

Three Bigfoot soldiers grabbed Albrecht and pinned him to his seat.

"This is idiotic!" screamed Albrecht.

Fireballs hit their helicopter again, and for a split second the interior of the craft was bathed in orange.

From his window Albrecht could see that the Greebo hanging from the second helicopter was focusing on them. It held out its arm, and a cluster of stubby missiles appeared.

"Missiles!" shouted Albrecht. "They have missiles!"

"This is stupid!" roared Timonen. "I'm going to land this helicopter if it's the last thing I do."

He removed his safety belt and was about to knock the pilot out of the way when a huge blast hit their craft. The massive troop helicopter dipped, its engines spluttering and kicking out balls of thick black smoke.

"We're going down!" shouted Buck. "Hold on!"

"Timonen!" cried Albrecht. "Buckle up!"

Saar hit him in the rear with his staff, forcing him back into his seat.

"Touch me again," said Timonen, "and even if we survive this, you won't!"

The helicopter went into an uncontrollable spin as its second propeller cut out.

"Here we go," shouted Albrecht, holding his breath as his head was sucked to the wall of the helicopter by G-force.

Saar closed his eyes, Timonen threw up, and the helicopter smashed into the ground. The world descended into darkness.

Albrecht awoke to the slimy sensation of a coyote licking his forehead

"Get off!" he blurted, batting its face away from his.

He unclipped his safety belt and peered around for other signs of life. The helicopter's roof was gone and lumps and bumps of snow-covered bodies surrounded him.

"Saar?" he said, scraping away at where he thought his friend had been sitting.

A few scoops of snow later, Saar's face was revealed.

"Are you all right?" he asked, lightly touching his nose. He could feel warm air blowing out of his nostrils.

Saar's eyes opened slowly and steadily. "We're alive?" he asked. "I was having the loveliest dream of snow-topped peaks and dancing foxes. I hoped it was the afterlife."

"You're very much alive," said Albrecht, clearing more snow from his friend's body. "You've been out cold for a while, though."

"And Timonen?" asked Saar.

Albrecht pointed to the biggest lump of snow a short distance from them. It was rising and falling gently.

"I'm surprised he's not snoring," said Albrecht.

"What about the others?" said Saar. He pulled his snow-covered staff out into the air.

"We'll soon find out," said Albrecht.

The two yetis quickly uncovered the Bigfoot troops and removed the snow from Timonen. Buck woke with a start as Albrecht unclipped his harness.

"Cold," he said, shivering. "Ice cold."

"It must be minus thirty at least," said Albrecht to Saar. "We need to get these guys moving before they freeze to death."

"Where's the other chopper?" asked Buck, his teeth chattering.

Albrecht couldn't see any sign of it. "It must have escaped," he said cautiously.

"We'll search for it later," said Buck. "For now we need to find our snow gear and some shelter."

Albrecht looked around, but most of the equipment that hadn't been held when the helicopter crashed was in pieces on the ground.

"I think your gear's pretty much done for," he said.

Buck rubbed his eyes and clutched his laser rifle.

"At least I've got protection," he said.

Albrecht looked at him with concern. "You sort out your troops and we'll scout the area for somewhere to get warm," he said.

He crunched over the snow to Saar and smoothed out a snowball in his palms.

"I'm not risking anything," he said, as he hurled the snowball at Timonen. It smashed straight into his face and exploded in a puff of wet spray.

"Monkeys!" shouted Timonen, snapping bolt upright in his chair with his hand raised in the air. As he realized he was awake and not dreaming about the jungle, he slumped down and looked at Albrecht.

"Who threw that?" he growled.

"How else was I supposed to wake you?" said Albrecht.

"Don't do it again," said Timonen.

"Fine," said Albrecht. "But we need your help, so get up and give us a hand."

Timonen tutted and ventured into an enormously long yawn.

"We landed then?" he said, unclipping his seatbelt and eyeing up the devastated helicopter.

Saar shook his head and walked out into the thick snow. They'd crashed on the edge of a mountain range sprinkled with pine trees. The pristine white landscape stretched for miles without any sign of human existence.

As Saar surveyed the land below, he saw plumes of mist and steam mingling with pockets of dense forest and ice-bound lakes and rivers. In among it all he caught sight of a thin tower of gray smoke rising into the air – a lone indicator of life in this harshest of environments. He called for Albrecht to take a closer look.

"We have fire," said Albrecht, zooming in close to the treetops with his binoculars. "And that's exactly what we need right now."

"You think it's Greebos?" asked Saar.

"I doubt it," said Albrecht. "They don't need warmth."

"Then maybe it's survivors from the other Bigfoot helicopter?" said Saar.

"Could be," said Albrecht hopefully.

The sky was gray with cloud and Albrecht sensed a snowfall was on its way. Their time was short.

"Round up the troops, Timonen!" said Albrecht. "There isn't much time."

Timonen grumpily obliged.

"Oi!" he shouted. "Buck, get over here with the rest of your Big Feet."

The Bigfoot division collected what remained of their gear and huddled together for warmth.

"We're Bigfoot," said Buck, as the group marched past Timonen.

"You can be whatever you like," he said in reply. "But you have two feet."

"Idiot," said Buck. He threw his rifle over his shoulder and shoved his hands under his armpits to keep them warm.

"What have you found?" he said to Albrecht.

Albrecht pointed down onto the plateau at the smoke.

"It's a bit of a trek," he said, lifting his backpack into its most comfortable position. "But where there's smoke, there's fire. And warmth."

"Right," said Buck, "let's make a start."

They moved off down the slope, skirting the edges of trees and surveying the area. The yetis were more than at home in the freezing conditions and pressed ahead to make a passage for the Bigfoot troops who followed close behind. There were no signs of Greebos or the other Bigfoot squad, but wolf tracks criss-crossed the deep snow. The land wasn't as empty as it appeared.

Tiny flakes of snow began to drop from the sky like dandruff, and steam from the yetis' mouths misted the air, blurring the few dark tree trunks that stood out from the snow. All was quiet and all was magical.

Albrecht walked through a clump of pines and entered a clearing full of mist. The mix of snow and steam erupting from a nearby hot spring made progress difficult. He wiped his brow and stepped carefully around the water so as not to fall in.

The light *crunch* of compacting snow made Albrecht freeze on the spot. The light had started to fade, but he could just make out a black shape emerging from the mist, white diamonds of ice and snow sparkling all over it.

"Who goes there?" asked Albrecht, bracing himself for conflict.

"Hey, man? You're no Bigfoot!" replied the creature. "What are you?"

The black shape drew closer, revealing itself to be a very tall Bigfoot. Albrecht relaxed.

"I'm a yeti," he said. "I'm Albrecht."

"A yeti?" said the Bigfoot. "Weird… Aren't you on the wrong continent?"

"I'm one of the Mythical 9th Division," he replied. "You're from the 6th, aren't you?"

"Whoa, no way, man," said the Bigfoot. "I'm no army man! I trained up, but I bailed."

He stretched out and shook Albrecht's hand.

"Oddball," he said.

"Oddball?" said Albrecht.

"That's my name," said the Bigfoot. "Don't wear it out."

"So if you're not in the 6th," said Albrecht, "then you don't know about the helicopter crash?"

"Nope," said Oddball. "I don't know about any crash. All I know is it's freezing out here. You want to get warm?"

"Me and about ten others," said Albrecht.

"Man that's almost a party," said Oddball. "Awesome. Bring them over!"

"Okaaaaay," said Albrecht cautiously. "I'll be with you in a minute."

"So you're Bigfoot?" said Balaclava, looking down from the back of his Greebo X. It thudded around the blackened room, stepping over streams of lava which coursed through the floor.

The Bigfoot prisoners, handcuffed and awaiting their fate, were survivors from the second helicopter. Their military training had taught them not to say a word to interrogators.

"I wish I got points for all the mythical creatures I've met," said Balaclava. "This world gets stranger by the day."

"We also intercepted another helicopter," said a Greeboid. "It's believed to have been destroyed."

"Destroyed?" said Balaclava. "How sure are you of that?"

The Greeboid looked towards the massive Greebo Xs that had captured the Bigfoot team.

"Eighty-five percent certain," said a Greebo X.

"Only eighty-five percent?" said Balaclava. "Who programmed you?"

"The super evil genius Balaclava," said the Greebo X.

"Exactly," replied Balaclava. "And your programming requires you to be one hundred percent sure. If the yetis aren't among these prisoners, you can be sure they're still out there."

"We shall return with proof of fatalities," said the Greebo X.

"Good," said Balaclava "There are times when an evil genius shouldn't have to do everything himself!"

Steam spurted from the back of the giant Greebos as they prepared to move.

"I want photos!" said Balaclava.

The Greebo Xs clunked out of the room, and Balaclava considered what to do with his prisoners. As an evil mastermind, he knew their fate would have to be devious, cunning and yet also terrible.

"I know," he said, patting his Greebo steed on its arm. "I have the perfect death for them."

"It's a Bigfoot," said Albrecht to the group, "but not as you'd know one."

"What do you mean?" said Buck, shivering violently. "He's not a civilian, is he?"

"He's not one of you, if that's what you mean," said Albrecht.

"Lazy slackers, the lot of them," said Buck.

"Maybe," said Albrecht, "but he's the one with the fire."

"Yeah," said Timonen, wandering off in the direction of Oddball's camp. "Probably got food, too. What are we waiting for?"

"He's right," said Saar. "Let's get you guys out of the cold."

"Follow me," said Albrecht.

As the sun set over the horizon, Albrecht and the others arrived at Oddball's home. Hidden deep in the forest, a huge rock rose out of the ground and created a perfect overhanging shelter. With fences of fallen pine trees and a wooden roof jutting out of the rock, it was homey, and just a little bit smelly. A roaring fire burned brightly outside the overhang, and Oddball directed his visitors to take seats around it.

The Bigfoot troops were much happier. The frost on their fur had melted to the ground and they could feel their fingers again.

"Put your feet up," said Oddball, bringing out some huge iron pots. "We've got to warm you up."

He pushed a metal rod into the fire and hung the pots from it, before filling them with water, vegetables and meat.

"Nothing like a good stew to get your temperature rising again," said Oddball.

Buck had been looking at him suspiciously.

"I know you," he said suddenly. "You were at my training camp. You're a deserter!"

"Hey," said Oddball, "I don't like that kind of talk around here."

Buck marched over and pressed his face up against Oddball's flat nose.

"Guys like you make me sick," said Buck, staring into the Bigfoot's face.

"If it wasn't for me, dude," said Oddball, stepping back, "you'd be out there in the cold tonight."

"Hey, hey, hey!" said Albrecht, forcing himself between the two. "Relax, Buck. We've got to get through this and the least you can do is be grateful for a warm fire."

"Listen to the yeti, dude," said Oddball.

"If you call me 'dude' once more," said Buck, "I'll make a fur coat out of you."

"Let's start again," said Albrecht.

Oddball shrugged.

"Fine by me," he said. "I don't care for this guy's bad vibes."

Buck returned to his seat, growling under his breath.

Timonen leaned over the pot, where the food was already bubbling.

"It smells good," he said.

"Won't be ready for a little while yet, though," said Oddball.

Timonen looked distraught. "Have you got any snacks to see me through?"

"Yeah, man," said Oddball, totally forgetting his argument with Buck. "I got munchies coming outta my ears." He pointed to a metal trunk standing against the rock. "In there, dude."

Timonen delved inside and found bags of crackers and corn chips.

"Where'd you get all this?" said Timonen, happier than ever.

"Trade secrets!" said Oddball, tapping his nose.

Timonen passed the bags around, making sure he had a fistful first.

"So," said Oddball. "What brings you guys around here?"

"The world is about to end," said Buck.

"Whoa," said Oddball. "Really?"

"Not quite," said Buck, "but it shows how little you care."

"Hey, man, lay off," said Oddball. "You're the one crashing my pad, remember."

"Buck, apologize," said Albrecht.

"Okay," said Buck, relenting. "Sorry."

"We're here because of the super volcano below Yellowstone," said Saar.

"Far out," said Oddball.

"There's an evil genius ready to make it erupt," said Albrecht.

"Super far out," said Oddball.

"It won't be so far out once the land around here is turned into a roaring pool of molten rock," said Buck. "The whole of America will be affected, most of it destroyed."

"Not cool," said Oddball.

"That's the first correct thing I've heard you say," said Buck.

"So you haven't seen any evil giant robots hanging around?" said Albrecht.

"You think he'd notice?" said Buck.

"Whoa, dude, enough already," said Oddball. "I see everything."

"Sure you do," said Buck.

"I'm fine-tuned to the movements of Earth," said Oddball. "I'm, like, totally at one with nature."

"You're fine-tuned to bowel movements maybe, but you wouldn't know nature if it bit you," said Buck.

"Do you want to hear what I've seen or not?" said Oddball.

"Yes," said Saar. "Shut up, Buck. Let him speak."

"Hey, thanks," said Oddball. "Much respect."

"So what have you seen?" said Albrecht.

"Far more humans out here than usual," said Oddball. "At least before the snows came."

"What sort of humans?" asked Albrecht. "Can you describe them?"

"Park Rangers, lumberjacks," said Oddball. "Lots of those beardy types driving around in big vehicles. They look pretty cool, you know, but I've had to be more careful than ever not to be seen."

"Beards..." said Saar.

"I told you," said Timonen.

Oddball looked confused.

"There's a high chance that those humans with beards were robots," said Albrecht, by way of explanation.

"Awesome," said Oddball. "Man, that's so cool."

"No, it's not cool," said Buck.

"So where did you see all these people?" asked Albrecht.

"All over the place," said Oddball. "Working at the lakes and hot springs, building cabins and putting fences around the geysers."

"What's a geyser?" asked Albrecht.

"A jet of steaming hot water, blasting out of the ground," said Saar. "Lava plus water equals geyser."

"If you ever need a bath," said Oddball, "they're perfect."

"I can't imagine you make much use of them," said Buck.

Oddball pretended not to hear.

"And that's Old Faithful – the most famous geyser here," he said, pointing to the map Albrecht had just taken from his backpack. "They've been building that massive place next to it for ages."

"Could that be his base?" said Albrecht.

"As good a guess as any," said Buck.

"Then that should be our first port of call," said Saar.

"You'll have to wait for sunrise," said Oddball. "It's death all the way out there."

"Even for a yeti?" said Saar.

"If you know the terrain, go for it," said Oddball. "But even if you don't fall into a scalding hot spring, you'll probably stumble across a grizzly's cave, or even a pack of wolves. Man, the creatures out there are *hungry* this time of year."

"That's not ideal," said Albrecht.

"It would seem sensible to stay here for the night," said Saar.

"Totally," said Oddball. "Put your feet up."

With a high-pitched *beep*, Albrecht's RoAR indicated there was an incoming call. He stood up and wandered to a quiet area under Oddball's rock.

"Captain Ponkerton," said Albrecht, removing his RoAR and holding it in front of his face.

"How are things?" asked the Captain.

"We were attacked by flying Greebos. Our helicopter went

down, but our team survived."

"Great," said Ponkerton. "That's all we need."

"What's happened?" said Albrecht.

"Grubchook has detected increased seismic activity in your area," he said. "I fear time is running out."

Albrecht banged his fist on the rock. "It's too dangerous for us to move," he said. "The weather's worse than on Everest."

"Albrecht," said Ponkerton, "the fate of millions is in your hands."

When Albrecht returned, Oddball was dishing up bowls of hot stew. The smell was delicious.

"We may not have the luxury of waiting for daybreak," said Albrecht. "There are increased signs of volcanic activity and our time is running out."

"I'm not moving," said Timonen. "Not till I've eaten."

"Are you sure it's safe out there?" said Saar.

"No," said Albrecht, "but I'd rather deal with snow than lava."

"My troops can't go anywhere in these conditions," said Buck.

"Then the Mythical 9th will have to go on ahead," said Albrecht. "Timonen, finish up."

"No way!" he said. "If the world's ending I don't want to be hungry."

"Saar?" said Albrecht. "Are you coming?"

"I don't think it's wise," he said. "Not even Balaclava would go out in this."

"But if we don't go we'll be up to our knees in lava before we find him," said Albrecht. "We can't sit around waiting for the world to blow up."

Saar mulled this over.

"I can't let you go alone," he said finally. "I'll come with you even if it's the death of us."

"I'm not changing my mind," said Timonen.

Albrecht handed a GRoWL to Timonen. "Contact us when you can," he said, "and stay close to the Bigfoot. They'll need you."

"I'll look after him," said Oddball. "If you're determined to go out in the dead of night, you should head for the road about a mile west."

"Keep safe," said Buck.

"Right," said Albrecht, saluting and walking off through the trees. "Until tomorrow."

Saar wrapped his scarf tightly about his neck and followed Albrecht.

"I hope you know what you're doing," said Saar.

"So do I," said Albrecht.

THE MYTHICAL 9th DIVISION

Chapter 9: Frosty the Yeti

AS THE SNOWFALL STOPS, YELLOWSTONE NATIONAL PARK IS LIT BY THE GLOW OF A THOUSAND STARS

158

"There's the road," said Albrecht, checking his map. "It'll lead us straight to those geysers. From there it's a straight two-hour trek to what might be Balaclava's base."

"Then let's hurry up," said Saar. "I can smell wolves nearby."

"We can't be scared of wolves," said Albrecht. "We've got a job to do."

"Wolves will hunt you until you can run no more," said Saar. "Then, as a pack, they'll bite your neck and bleed you to death before tearing the limbs from your body."

"Okay. I'm suitably scared now," said Albrecht, quickening his pace. "Thanks."

"I was just saying—" said Saar.

A loud *whoosh*ing noise shook the ground beside them and a thick plume of steam fizzed into the air, followed by a tower of scalding water. Albrecht skipped a step and almost tumbled into the snow.

"More geysers," said Saar angrily.

"They're everywhere!" said Albrecht. "I wish they'd give you some warning."

As the jet of water died down, the howls of wolves pierced the night air.

"Terrific," said Albrecht.

He withdrew his binoculars from his backpack, switched them to night vision and scoured the land. He found the creatures trotting alongside the forest's edge.

"There's at least twelve," said Albrecht, his heart starting to race. "They're heading our way."

"I suppose we should run," said Saar.

"There's no suppose about it!" cried Albrecht.

They went as fast as they could, leaping over rocks and fallen trees and avoiding the numerous thermal springs that steamed in the nighttime air.

Albrecht checked the RoAR for directions as he ran.

"How much further?" shouted Saar, using his staff to vault over a stream.

"We're almost there!" said Albrecht.

The wolves were gaining, their cries growing louder and louder.

"Just through this clearing!" he said.

Saar could almost feel the wolves' breath on his legs. He couldn't see them, as they darted in and out of the tree line behind him, but he could sense they were just yards away.

Suddenly a blazing searchlight crossed the ground a short distance ahead, traveling across the snow and whipping over the treetops before cutting back to re-trace its path.

"There!" said Albrecht, picking up the pace. He could see a square black shadow above the silhouetted treetops.

Dodging the searchlight's beam, the yetis veered from the covered road and vanished into the forest. Tree trunks flashed past in a blur, and without any warning, Albrecht and Saar ran headfirst into a solid wall.

"If it's not geysers and wolves it's indescribable blocks of metal!" said Saar, clutching his shoulder.

"Grrr," muttered Albrecht, shaking his head.

Saar slumped to the ground. He held out his staff and it started to glow blue, illuminating the area around them.

"Here they come…" he said.

Pairs of small glowing eyes were hovering in front of them, reflecting the light from his staff. Growling and slobbering, the wolves were preparing to attack.

Albrecht banged the metal wall.

"We're done for," he said.

"There's always a way out," said Saar. "Always."

A puff of exhaust fumes escaped from the metal wall, and with a growl, it started to shake. Albrecht pressed his hand to the metal. He could barely breathe from the fumes, but he had a very good feeling about things.

"We're saved!" he said, grabbing Saar by the scarf and wrenching him up.

The wall started to move, kicking dirt and snow into the air.

"It's a tank!" said Albrecht.

The vehicle moved off, grinding its way through the forest and out into the clearing. Albrecht carefully climbed up its side, trying to make as little noise as possible, and with a helping hand, Saar was soon alongside. They toppled over onto its roof and breathed a sigh of relief.

"This is one of Balaclava's snow tanks," whispered Albrecht, lying low to evade detection.

"A much safer option than a pack of wolves," said Saar.

"Far, far safer," said Albrecht.

Once the tank reached the snowbound road, it upped a gear and powered off at incredible speed.

"And wherever it's taking us," said Albrecht, "it's got to be going the right way."

The tank traveled for a short while, passing numerous steaming geysers and clusters of bison huddled together to keep out the cold. Eventually they reached a steel-fenced enclosure. Gates opened to let the tank through and Albrecht and Saar spied scores of Greeboids, rushing around with clipboards. Six tanks lined the edges of the enclosure and two giant Greebo Xs stomped back and forth with their flamethrowers primed. At the top of a huge pylon sat the searchlight that had been scouring the land.

"What are they doing?" whispered Albrecht.

Saar pointed across to one of Balaclava's tanks. It had a drill on its front, just like the one they'd seen in Antarctica. It was tilted downward, ready to go.

With the blast of steaming water from a geyser at the center of the enclosure, a siren sounded and the Greeboids retreated to the safety of the tanks. With its engine fired up, the drill tank's nose cut into the earth. Mud and snow piled up around it and within seconds it was gone from the surface.

"What can we do?" said Albrecht.

A muffled explosion rocked the ground and shockwaves rippled through the snow.

"I fear we're too late for anything," said Saar. "We don't stand a chance."

"If it's the end of everything," said Albrecht, "I love you, Saar. You've been a brother to me."

"More a father, I like to think," he replied hesitantly.

Albrecht gripped Saar's hand and squeezed it tight.

"I'm not your real father," said Saar, frowning.

"Just in case," said Albrecht. "Just in case…"

The next second, the drill tank burst back through the ground and tilted down to horizontal, followed by a trail of blisteringly hot lava. The yetis waited for the end, but nothing much happened.

"Weird," said Albrecht.

"It's not the explosive finale I was expecting," said Saar.

A Greeboid, clipboard in one hand and walkie-talkie in the other, climbed out of a tank and walked over to the lava flow.

"Third and final perimeter charge unleashed," he said. "The caldera is weakening and ready for the Magma Bomb."

Balaclava's voice crackled over the radio.

"Excellent," he said. "Good work! Return to base. Countdown T minus six hours."

"Yes, sir," said the Greeboid.

Albrecht could barely contain his relief.

"Did you hear that?" he whispered to Saar. "We're not too late!"

"They're weakening Earth's crust," said Saar, "ready to blow it sky high."

"With a Magma Bomb!" finished Albrecht.

The tanks' engines ignited and thick exhaust fumes spurted out of their rears.

"We may still have time to save the world," said Albrecht.

"Six hours to go," said Saar.

"And finally we know what we're dealing with," said Albrecht.

"So maybe you should let go of my hand now?" said Saar.

"Right," said Albrecht.

"Right," said Saar, reclaiming his hand as his own.

The yetis kept low on the tank as it plowed for an hour across the snow to a wide-open area. The moon's glow reflected off a frothing tower of water, which sparkled like fairy dust in the dark.

"Old Faithful," said Albrecht.

"What time is it?" said Saar.

"About five…" said Albrecht.

"Make a note," said Saar. "It fires up almost like clockwork."

The tank now switched on its headlights, revealing a flurry of activity in the distance. Giant Greebos patrolled the area and ushered the tank along like parking lot attendants. The large building that they'd seen on the map stood high in the distance, but the tank turned away from that direction.

"Head down," whispered Albrecht.

The tank stopped in front of a wide metal trapdoor hidden in the forest floor, which opened on hydraulic lifts. A bright red light shone from below ground and the tank's engine revved up once more.

"Are we going in?" said Saar.

"Too right we are!" said Albrecht. "Hang on!"

The tank powered inside, down a steep slope and into a huge metal hangar filled with parked tanks. The building was cavernous, with a furious mix of black metal beams and burning streams of lava crisscrossing the floor like a spider's web. Steam and smoke lilted through the air, blurring the yetis' view. Saar wrapped his scarf tightly about his face, with his eyes poking out of the top.

"Why did you do that?" said Albrecht.

Saar pointed to the streams of red lava on the floor.

"Lava," he said. "Toxic fumes aren't good for us…"

"Oh, great," said Albrecht.

"Just don't breathe very often," said Saar.

The intense heat was deeply uncomfortable and the yetis started to sweat. As the tank door opened, they slipped down to the ground, hidden by the tank tracks.

"Muster in Assembly Room One," said a Greeboid, climbing down from the tank's roof. Two other robots followed him and they headed off through the base.

"We should go after them," said Albrecht, starting to choke. The air tasted foul. "Rotten eggs!" he coughed.

"It's sulfur," said Saar. "We can't stay here long."

"I couldn't agree more," said Albrecht.

They were about to set off after the Greeboids when a huge set of iron doors at the far end of the hangar squealed open.

Two Greebo Xs stomped through the doorway with the Bigfoot prisoners pacing mournfully behind them. They were still handcuffed and their legs were bound together so they formed a chain gang. Two Greeboids brought up the rear, reading charts from their clipboards and discussing the best angles to drill into the earth.

Albrecht and Saar were hesitating, unsure of their next move, when the doors burst open again, and Balaclava appeared on the back of his Greebo X. The yetis froze.

"He's here!" mouthed Albrecht silently, as the giant Greebo passed them by.

He waited a few seconds, then, using the line of tanks for cover, shuffled from one to the next, until he had a perfect view. As the yetis watched, Balaclava's drill tank opened and the Bigfoot troops were herded inside. The two Greeboids followed them in, closing the door over their heads.

"What are they doing with the Bigfoot troops?" whispered Albrecht.

"And what's that cylinder thing attached to the back?" said Saar.

Balaclava's Greebo X took him to the cylinder, and the evil genius cast his eye over a number of pipes on its top. From up high he was able to lean over and type a code into the numerical display.

"Engaging the volcanic rods," said Balaclava.

He pressed a final button and six metal rods, their ends exposed from the sides of the cylinder, started to move inwards.

"The Magma Bomb is primed," said Balaclava, laughing maniacally. "Only four hours to the end of the world!"

His Greebo fired streams of flame into the air in celebration as the tank drove off through the hangar to the exit. The two Greebo Xs followed it like a pair of loyal servants.

Balaclava's Greebo disappeared through the iron doors and was soon out of view.

"What are we going to do?" said Albrecht. "That tank is carrying the Magma Bomb and there's no way we can fight those robots."

"Get Timonen," said Saar. "We need as much help as possible."

Albrecht took out his RoAR, but the signal was completely dead.

"Must be this bunker blocking the reception," said Albrecht. "We're on our own and we've got to follow that tank. There's got to be a way of stopping it."

THE MYTHICAL 9th DIVISION

Chapter 10: Oddball the Great

As soon as the sun rose over the mountains and light filtered in through the forest, Timonen stirred. The night had been very cold and most of the Bigfoot team had ended up in a great big huddle to keep warm. Timonen had slept against their backs, stealing their heat. Now, with an enormous stretch and yawn, he sat upright.

"Hey, man," said Oddball, stoking the fire. "You're awake. Coffee?"

"Ooh," said Timonen. "Don't mind if I do."

"Don't stick too close to these dudes," said Oddball. "I can tell you're different. You like to take things easy."

"Too right," said Timonen.

"When there's a problem in the world," said Oddball, passing over a cup full of hot black coffee, "the first thing I say to myself is, 'Relax, take it easy. Think things over first.'"

"That's what I'm always trying to tell Albrecht. He never listens to me."

"Oh, man," said Oddball. "You gotta change his outlook, dude. He'll die young of … of worry or something."

Timonen slugged back the coffee. "That's gooooood," he said.

"Life out here is sweet," said Oddball. "It gets icy in winter, but apart from that it's bliss. The Mythical 6th just wasn't for me."

"You're making me jealous," said Timonen, staring up at beams of light filtering through the trees. "The others are always telling me what to do."

"That's so bogus, dude," said Oddball.

"Yeah," said Timonen. "If they're not waking me up, they're throwing me out of airplanes or starving me half to death."

"Maybe you should do something about it, man," said Oddball. "Don't stand for that treatment."

"Not even my sister Tum-Tum bossed me around this much," said Timonen.

The Bigfoot laughed.

"Don't say another thing," he said. "I know how it is."

"Yeah, you've got it good," said Timonen.

"That's life as a free creature," said Oddball. "I can wash as little as I like, sleep as much as I want... If that's how you feel, you've gotta get out, dude."

Timonen was never one to feel overly worried about things, but Oddball was really making him think.

"Why *do* I work for the Mythical 9th Division?" he said. "What does it do for me?"

"Only you can answer that question," said Oddball wisely.

"Hmm," said Timonen, thinking. He sat back, breathing in the crisp, fresh air. It was heavenly.

Suddenly a sizzling ball of fire burst through the pine trees and exploded on the floor near the pile of Bigfoot soldiers. Buck leapt to attention, Oddball fell on his back, and Timonen jumped into tree cover as a second fireball surged through the trees.

"We're under attack!" shouted Buck. "Take evasive action!"

Three Greebo Xs came flying through the tree canopy, scorching the forest floor with flamethrowers before they slammed into the ground. Their heads turned left and right, processing the number of enemies they faced.

"My home!" cried Oddball. His shelter was burning with such ferocity that melted water was gushing from the treetops.

"They've come back to finish the job," said Buck. "Let's show them what we're made of."

The Bigfoot team surrounded the Greebos, clutching their laser rifles tightly in their hands. One Bigfoot searched frantically around the forest floor for his missing weapon, and Oddball thought very briefly about handing back the one he'd stolen. But now clearly wasn't the time.

"Erm, Buck…" said Timonen.

"Not now, big guy," said Buck. "On the count of three."

The soldiers raised their rifles.

"One… Two…"

"Buck, the lasers don't—"

"Three!"

In an instant, bright-blue rays ricocheted off the Greebo armor and flew straight back at the Bigfoot division, scattering them over the ground as they plunged for cover. Timonen ducked to the ground, reaching out to pull Oddball to safety.

"The lasers don't work!" yelled Buck.

"No kidding," muttered Timonen.

Buck swept his hair back over his head and swallowed hard. He loved the excitement of battle. "Form attack teams. Three per robot! Let's do this with our hands!"

The Greebos stomped into a triangular formation to cover their backs. "Attack!" shouted Buck.

The Bigfoot division charged as torrents of fire burst from the Greebos' weapons. The onslaught was terrible.

"Retreat!" shouted Buck.

The Bigfoot team ran into the forest, with the Greebos close behind.

Timonen crawled out from his hiding place and put a finger to his lips. "Shhh," he whispered to Oddball.

They hid behind tree trunks while the Greebos disappeared from view, knocking down trees and setting them alight as they progressed.

"That's so uncool…" mumbled Oddball.

Timonen loosened his grip and stood up. Oddball's camp was a scorched wasteland. Timonen growled and tore a broken tree stump out of the ground. He threw it at the huge rock.

"I hate those robots," he said.

"Yeah, man," said Oddball. "Me too. They've destroyed my supplies."

The metal canister where he stored his snacks had melted under the blazing heat and was now just a glowing lump.

"No more Mr. Nice Guy," said Timonen, growling under his breath. "It's time to finish those robots for good."

"Look, dude," said Oddball. "I know I'm not an army man,

but I might be able to help you."

"What have you got?" asked Timonen. "Bazooka arms?"

Oddball negotiated a clump of burning branches.

"Over here, man," he said.

Timonen watched Oddball unhook a rope tied to a metal hoop on the floor. Three pine trees swung into the air, taking with them a mass of dried foliage and camouflage nets.

"I don't have bazookas in my arms," said Oddball, "but I do have this…"

Timonen was lost for words. If he'd been a cartoon character his eyes would have shot out on stalks.

"That's exactly what we need," he said, stamping his foot. "And it's reminds me exactly why I like being in the Mythical 9th Division!"

Albrecht and Saar slipped out into the crisp morning air, close behind the Magma Bomb. The hangar door eased shut and they threw themselves into cover behind tall pine trees. The rumbling of tanks in the distance made them incredibly uneasy.

"I hate to say it," growled Saar, "but we're really out of our depth here."

"Can't your yeti powers help?" said Albrecht desperately.

"You fail to understand the Way of the Yeti," said Saar. "It's a protective, benevolent power."

"Not one to knock out an army of tanks and robots then?" said Albrecht.

"I'm afraid not," said Saar.

Albrecht signaled to move out and scrambled through the trees to the clearing they'd driven through last night.

"Just look," said Albrecht. "There are at least thirty robots and too many tanks to count."

"And sitting here at ground zero," said Saar, "we'd be vaporized in seconds."

Albrecht removed his backpack and opened every compartment. There was nothing that might help the situation. He held his RoAR and realized the signal had returned.

"Help me, Timonen," he said, "you're my only hope."

THE MYTHICAL 9th DIVISION

Chapter 11: Tanks, But No Tanks

ALBRECHT TRIES TO CONTACT TIMONEN ON THE RoAR

COME IN, TIMONEN! OVER...

YEAH. I'M DRIVING A TANK!

BRRRRMM

"**Y**ou're driving a tank?" said Albrecht. "Where did you get a tank from?"

"Oddball stole it," said Timonen.

"Hey, man!" said Oddball, standing at the cannon placed on top of the tank. "I only borrowed it!"

"Whatever," said Albrecht. "We could use a tank, right here, right now."

"How come?" said Timonen, shifting gears and directing the tank through a burning hole in the forest.

"They're preparing to detonate the volcano," said Albrecht. "There are tanks and Greebos crawling all over the place."

"We need you," said Saar.

"Aw," said Timonen. "Really?"

"Really," said Albrecht.

"I'll be there," said Timonen. His friends' words had brought tears to his eyes. "Just give me a minute, I've got to rescue our Bigfoot friends first."

"What happened?" said Albrecht.

"Hey, dude!" cried Oddball. "Greebos up ahead!"

His fingers tightened around the trigger on the cannon's handle.

"Long story," said Timonen to Albrecht. "Anyway, like I said, must dash."

He put down the GRoWL and searched for the Greebos through the tiny window at the front of the tank. One was flying through the air over the trees, searching for the Bigfoot troops, while the other two were burning vegetation to clear their path.

"Right," shouted Timonen, driving straight for them. "How's your shot?"

"Not bad," said Oddball.

The Bigfoot aimed and fired at the flying Greebo. Three fireballs blasted out, shaking the tank. Two of them deflected off the robot's armor, but one of them hit its rocket

boosters. It veered off course with
its jets spluttering and wheez-
ing, and with a puff of smoke it
crashed to the ground.

"YEEHAAW!" cried
Oddball.

"Good shot!" said Timonen,
punching the roof.

A group of Bigfoot
rushed out of the forest to
see what had brought down the
robot. Oddball saluted from the gun
turret.

"I've never stolen anything as good as this," said Timonen.

"I didn't steal it!" said Oddball. "It's borrowed…"

The two remaining Greebos turned to face the tank.

"Right," said Timonen, accelerating faster. "Come and get us."

Oddball fired at the Greebos, but the fireballs evaporated on
the robots' chests.

"Oh, man," said Oddball. "These guys are tough."

Timonen drove straight towards them.

"Aim for their eyes," said Timonen. "That's usually a bad-die's weakness."

Oddball focused the gun sight as the Greebos let loose with their flamethrowers. When those didn't work, they opened their arms to reveal clusters of missiles.

"Incoming!" shouted Timonen.

Missiles flew into the ground in front of the tank, exploding with enough force to kick it briefly into the air. It thudded back to the ground undamaged.

"What is this thing made of?" said Timonen in amazement. "I love it!"

With the Greebo Xs occupied by Timonen and Oddball, the Bigfoot team mounted an attack. Buck took the lead and leapt onto the nearest robot's back.

"Don't fire!" yelled Timonen to Oddball.

Oddball swung the turret upwards to face the blue sky.

"Relax, dude!" he shouted.

Buck had no intention of letting go of his Greebo, but the robot wasn't going down easily. It swung its top half around and around to dislodge the Bigfoot soldier, with no effect. Buck reared up high over its head and smashed his rifle butt onto its metal skull. A few sparks leapt out of its neck joints, but it only served to anger the robot more. It fired missiles recklessly into the air in response.

"That's it!" said Timonen, realizing the robot's weakness. "Its neck!"

"Oddball, get down here!" ordered Timonen. "They need my help!"

Oddball ducked inside the tank and took the controls as Timonen pulled himself out onto the roof. He dodged a stream of fire and shouted out to Buck.

"Pull their heads off!" he cried. "Their necks are weak!"

He watched frustratedly as the Bigfoot struggled to finish off the Greebos.

"Get me closer," he said, banging on the roof.

As soon as Timonen was within reach he jumped high into the air and landed slap-bang on top of Buck's Greebo.

"Like this!" said Timonen, muscling his way to the robot's neck.

His massive palms gripped the head. He tugged, he growled and grumbled, he toiled and turned and – finally – with a colossal twist of his massive palms, Timonen tore the Greebo's head clean off.

"By the power of the yeti!" he screamed, tossing it into the forest like a football.

Buck was stunned and the Bigfoot soldiers pulling at the second Greebo upped their game, pooling their strength for one final effort. With a primal roar, the team severed the robot's head and held it aloft as sparks showered to the ground.

"Right!" said Timonen, showing a level of leadership that would have made Albrecht proud. "Get on the tank, we've got the world to save."

With his entourage of battle-hardened Bigfoot at his side, Timonen got back in the tank.

"Come on, Oddball," said Timonen. "Albrecht and Saar need help."

"Right on, man!" said Oddball, stepping on the gas.

• • •

"Get me the president of the United States," said Balaclava.

He was standing next to Old Faithful and a Greeboid was filming him with a video camera. Another Greeboid was standing nearby, holding a computer display.

"We're live!" said the Greeboid. "Signal incoming!"

The display fizzed from black to showing the American flag before reverting to the president in the Oval Office.

"Mr. President!" said Balaclava. "I thought you'd like a ringside seat to the hottest show in the world!"

"What is this insolence?" said the president. "Who are you?"

"My name is Balaclava," said Balaclava. "And I'm being courteous, not insolent. I was under the impression you'd like to see what was going to destroy your country."

"Destroy America?" said the president. "I don't know who you think you are, but this has to stop now."

"It's too late for that," said Balaclava.

"Too late?" snapped the president. "But this is the first I've heard of it."

"That's what happens when you fail to reply to answering machine messages!" said Balaclava. He pointed to the cylinder attached to the back of his drill tank. "Say hello to the Magma Bomb."

"Bomb!" exclaimed the president.

"And the countdown has begun!" said Balaclava proudly. "In ten minutes' time the Magma Bomb will detonate in the super volcano under Yellowstone National Park, causing an eruption big enough to destroy at least half of the United States."

"This is madness," said the president. "And wholly unnecessary. Can we not talk this through?"

"You had your chance," said Balaclava. "Besides, your Bigfoot regiment have made matters even worse."

The president turned away from the camera and spoke to an adviser. He was unaware of the mythical divisions.

"Hey!" said Balaclava angrily. "Don't turn away! Look at me when I'm talking to you!"

The president's focus returned to the screen.

"Mr. Balaclava," said the president, "I believe we can negotiate. If you can just give me time—"

But Balaclava was far too incensed for that.

"You have but a short amount of time left on Earth," he

yelled at the camera. "Make the most of it!"

The Greeboid stopped filming.

"They'll be sorry they never paid me my due," said Balaclava, climbing onto the back of his Greebo X. "To the bunker," he said.

"Albrecht!" said Ponkerton through Albrecht's RoAR. "Come in, Albrecht!"

Albrecht switched on the RoAR's screen and Ponkerton's face flickered into view.

"Ten minutes to the end of the world!" said Ponkerton, a bead of sweat trickling down his forehead. "Tell me you've got the situation in hand."

"We're on top of things…" he said, lying.

Saar scratched his chin and looked at Albrecht in disbelief.

"Good," said Ponkerton. "I've just had an angry, and frankly, very scared president of the United States on the phone."

"Leave it to us," said Albrecht.

"I know you'll pull through," said Ponkerton. "Over and out."

The RoAR's screen went black.

"Get Timonen on the line," said Saar.

Albrecht called the GRoWL.

"Hey, dude!" said a cheerful voice. "Oddball here."

"Where are you?" said Albrecht. "Where's Timonen?"

"He's driving," he replied. "We're on our way, man. What's the hurry?"

Albrecht's attention was taken by the sound of drilling. The tank carrying the Magma Bomb had started boring down into the ground beside Old Faithful.

"THE HURRY?" shouted Albrecht. "We've got ten minutes until we're blown sky high, so just get here now!" He slammed the RoAR into his backpack.

"Let's think," said Saar, who was also feeling the pressure. "No matter how strong a tank is, it always has an Achilles heel."

"And that is?" said Albrecht.

"It's usually weaker at its back," said Saar. "We need to target its exhaust."

He looked around hopelessly for any sign of Timonen and the Bigfoot troops. There wasn't even a sniff of them on the air.

"We're going to have to do this ourselves," said Albrecht.

"Against tanks and missile-bearing robots?" said Saar.

"I admit they're not great odds," said Albrecht.

"But we've known worse," said Saar.

Albrecht started to count.

"One, two, three…"

"Run!" shouted Saar.

They immediately caught the attention of two giant Greebos. Rockets flew in their direction and exploded into the ground. Soil, rock and snow catapulted into the air.

Two tanks revved their engines and drove together to block the yetis' path. Saar pole-vaulted over their tops with his staff and Albrecht was left to climb up and across. Two Greeboids clambered through the manholes of each tank and took control of the gun turrets. Fireballs blasted out, singeing Albrecht's backpack as he leapt to the ground.

"Get in the hole!" shouted Albrecht, held up by an exploding rocket. He dived into its crater for cover.

Greebos and tanks scrambled furiously, fireballs sizzled through the air and rockets zoomed overhead as Saar dropped into the gaping tunnel left by the drill tank. He chased down into the dark following the glow of the tank's headlights. He could see exhaust fumes pumping out of the bottom right of the vehicle.

It was drilling down at such a rate Saar struggled to keep up. The Magma Bomb wobbled and shook on its descent and Saar grabbed hold of its casing, suddenly aware of how large it was close up.

"Fleas of a yak," he said, eyeing up the mass of tiny pipes and panels on its side. The Magma Bomb's digital counter was ticking down.

"7:45," said Saar. "7:44."

The temperature was rising rapidly. Saar pulled at his scarf, allowing some heat to escape, when inspiration hit him. His scarf had a mithril core. If anything could stop the tank it was his *scarf*.

With mud and water spraying around him, he unlooped the scarf from his neck and rolled it up as tight as he could.

"I hope this works," he said, jumping forward onto the back of the tank. He could see the exhaust port protruding from its base, next to the tirelessly churning tank track.

In one deft movement, Saar swooped low and stuffed his scarf into the exhaust. It immediately stopped expelling fumes.

"Right," he said, clutching at his staff and hanging on to the tank for dear life. "Let's see what that does."

Albrecht clawed his way out of the crater to find himself surrounded. Tanks aimed their gun turrets at him and Greebo Xs stood with their flamethrowers ready to fire. He raised his hands in surrender. There was no way out.

"All right," he said, exhausted. "Do your worst."

A Greebo X moved to strike when an explosion sent tons of dirt and smoke flying from the tunnel.

"Oh, no!" cried Albrecht. "Saar!"

The Greebos rushed to the edge of the tunnel and peered down into the darkness.

"Is that it?" said Albrecht. "Is that the end?"

———— 9th ————

Chapter 12: What a Geyser!

203

204

"**Y**ou took your time!" said Albrecht.

Timonen threw him over his shoulder and charged over the tanks blocking the path. A searing fireball hit the ground, its fire bursting over Timonen's back. He stumbled briefly, then found his feet.

"You all right?" asked Albrecht.

"Just a scratch," said Timonen, breathing through the pain. "Where's Saar?"

"Down the hole, over there!" said Albrecht. "But we might be too late."

Timonen saw faint wisps of smoke threading out of the tunnel. "Not yet we aren't," he said.

He barged his way through a scrum of Greeboids and pelted down the tunnel with Albrecht still held tight.

"We'll get him," said Timonen.

Within a minute they'd caught up with the tank, which had stopped moving. They found Saar caked in soot and poring over the Magma Bomb, trying to figure out its wiring.

"Help!" he said, coughing.

The Magma Bomb was starting to glow red.

"We've got four minutes!" said Saar. "We have to deactivate it!"

Timonen dropped Albrecht and pried the tank door open with his fingers. Inside the brightly lit cockpit stood the two Greeboids, looking puzzled as to why the tank had stopped. The Bigfoot prisoners were sitting on the floor, handcuffed to each other.

Albrecht pushed his way inside and grabbed the Greeboids, one in each hand.

"Stop the bomb!" he said, snarling.

The robots' eyes turned red and angry.

"Magma Bomb unstoppable," they said in unison, their voices reverting to robot speak.

"It can't be!" growled Albrecht.

"Albrecht," said Saar, trying not to panic. "The tunnel's

filling with hot water."

Albrecht thumped the two Greeboids' heads together and they sparked. The lights went out in their eyes and they crumpled to the floor.

"Timonen, set free the prisoners while I help Saar," said Albrecht.

The Magma Bomb was starting to shake and Saar didn't seem any closer to understanding it.

"There must be a way to stop it," said Albrecht feverishly.

"I've defused bombs before, but this is something else," said Saar.

Albrecht suddenly felt a burning sensation on his feet.

"Argh!" he said. "This water's boiling!"

It was also rising by the second. Saar realized why.

"Get everyone out of here!" he said. "Now!"

"What?" yelled Albrecht. "We're not leaving you."

"Do it!" said Saar.

Timonen appeared from the tank, followed by the Bigfoot troops.

"Go!" said Saar. He climbed over to the side of the vehicle.

"Less than a minute to go! RUN!"

"But—" said Albrecht.

"I have a plan!" said Saar. "Now go."

Albrecht clutched Saar's arm one last time then jumped across the water. He ran up the tunnel as fast as he could, with Timonen and the Bigfoot team hard on his heels.

The timer fell to twenty seconds as Saar unlatched the Magma Bomb from the tank. The bomb settled on the top of the water, which was now bubbling and steaming more intensely than ever.

"Old Faithful," said Saar. "Don't let me down…"

Saar caught hold of the bomb and climbed on top of it. He clung on with one eye shut and the other focused on the counter, steadily decreasing to zero. He looked up to see Albrecht and the others leave the tunnel, then his eye returned to the counter.

10 … 9 … 8…

The water continued to rise.

7 … 6 … 5…

Saar started to worry. A lot.

4 … 3…

With an enormous roar, the water level surged from below, and Saar went shooting up the tunnel at breakneck speed. Like a bullet from a gun Saar shot out into the daylight and released the Magma Bomb. He crashed to the ground in a heap of fur, as the bomb powered further into the air on a spout of water.

BOOOOOOOOM!

The explosion could be heard for miles around. Birds scattered into the air. Wolves howled. Bison sat down.

Albrecht leaned back on a tank, his head pounding. The spray from Old Faithful was drifting over his fur. Captain Ponkerton was on the RoAR.

"Balaclava," said Ponkerton. "Where is he?"

"We can't find him," said Albrecht. "The door to his bunker is sealed and we can't break it."

"Well," said Ponkerton, "at least he can't escape, even if we have to wait a lifetime for him to appear."

"That was our thought as well," said Albrecht.

"And you're all fine?" said Ponkerton.

"Pretty much," said Albrecht. "A few singed hairs, but nothing too worrying."

"Then if the world is safe once more," said Ponkerton, "take a breather before heading back to LEGENDS HQ with Buck. I'm afraid they're still talking about punishment and court-martial."

"You're kidding, right?" said Albrecht.

"Unfortunately not," said Ponkerton. "But I'm certain they'll go easy on you after you saved the world."

"That's kind of them," muttered Albrecht.

"I'll put in a good word, too," said Ponkerton. "For now, get some rest. The clear-up troops will be landing shortly. They'll take over from here."

Albrecht saluted.

"Over and out," said Ponkerton.

"Wow, man," said Oddball, walking past with a cup of coffee in his hand. "That explosion was out of this world!"

Saar was tending to his scorched feet on the floor.

"We were lucky," he said. "We've got Old Faithful to thank."

"Nature saved the day," said Oddball.

Buck and his troops marched alongside, many of them carrying Greebo X heads as trophies. They stopped and stomped to attention.

"Stand down, men," said Buck. He looked at Albrecht and offered his hand in peace. "I doubted you guys, but you proved yourselves worthy wingmen."

"And now you know how to stop massive robots," said Timonen, poking his head around the side of the tank. He walked over, awkwardly.

"What's the matter?" said Buck. "You hurt your legs?"

"Have you not seen his wounds?" said Saar.

"Huh?" said Buck.

"It's nothing," said Timonen, embarrassed, "just a flesh wound."

Albrecht sniggered.

Timonen turned around and pointed to his slightly burned, fur-free backside.

"Man," said Oddball laughing, "you look like a baboon!"

Buck started to laugh.

"Looks like there'll be a full moon tonight," he said.

"Yeah, yeah," said Timonen. "Keep 'em coming. There's enough of my backside for all of you."

214

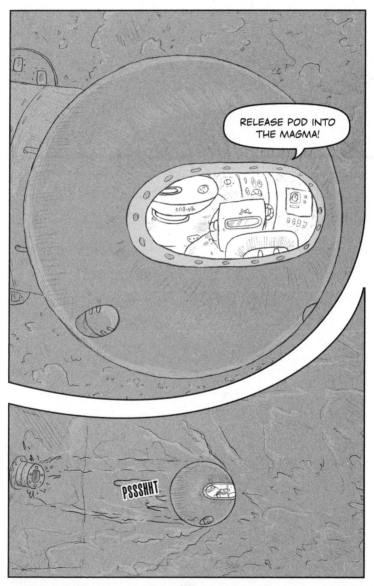

215

THE
END

THE MYTHICAL **9th** DIVISION

Appendix: The Founding of the Mythical 6th Division

The Bigfoot has long played an active role in the protection of the United States of America, with the first official mention of the creature dating to 1854: a simple note on a government receipt records "Salt beef for our Bigfoot allies."

While this fails to reveal how and why the Bigfoot were helping the government, we do have more substantial evidence from a decade later. A newly discovered photograph from 1862 shows a Bigfoot standing alongside Abraham Lincoln. At the height of the Civil War, Bigfoot were clearly aiding the president, probably in some capacity for the secret service.

It wasn't until the beginning of the twentieth century that the Bigfoot took a more permanent position within the U.S.

The early days of the Human-Bigfoot Alliance:
Abraham Lincoln meets a Bigfoot.

armed forces, with the creation of the Special Sasquatch Service in 1923. The SSS was led by a human named Evelyn Everhard, who lobbied for Bigfoot participation in all future armed conflicts. Their survival skills were so widely praised that much of their knowledge of forest lore was quickly incorporated into army training manuals.

The Second World War saw the Bigfoot's most widespread use, when the SSS secretly entered occupied France in advance of D-Day on June 6, 1944. Their skill in forest combat bolstered the Allied Forces, particularly during the Battle of the Bulge, and it is thought that they helped secure Hitler's Eagle's Nest mountain retreat at Berchtesgaden. Some graffiti reportedly made by Bigfoot troops can still be seen in woodwork inside the building.

With the birth of LEGENDS in 1945, the SSS was rebranded the Mythical 6th Division, which forms the backbone of secret missions where forest terrain is a hazard. Now commanded by Captain Winston Everhard, Evelyn's grandson, the division continues to thrive and has earned its reputation as the hardest working of all LEGENDS' defense squads.

9th

ALEX MILWAY HAS
ALWAYS ENJOYED MAKING
UP STORIES, AND AFTER LEAVING
ART COLLEGE, HE DISCOVERED THAT
HE LIKED TO WRITE AND ILLUSTRATE THEM
AS WELL. HIS INTEREST IN FURRY
CREATURES FIRST REARED ITS HEAD IN
THE MOUSEHUNTER TRILOGY, WHERE
WEIRD AND WONDERFUL MICE RAN RIOT ALL
OVER THE WORLD. WITH *THE MYTHICAL 9TH
DIVISION*, THE FUR QUOTA GOT EVEN BIGGER,
AS HE HAD TO MASTER THE ART OF DRAWING A
TROOP OF YETIS WHOSE MAIN PURPOSE WAS TO
SAVE THE WORLD. ALEX IS NOW A FULL-TIME
AUTHOR-ILLUSTRATOR, WHO SUFFERS FROM
FURBALLS AND WORKS FROM HIS
HOME IN LONDON.

IN THE MOUNTAINS OF WALES, SOMETHING STRANGE IS HAPPENING. IT SHOULD BE THE MIDDLE OF SUMMER, BUT SNOWDONIA HAS BEEN BESIEGED BY BLIZZARDS AND ICE STORMS. THE ARCTIC-TRAINED SOLDIERS SENT TO INVESTIGATE HAVE DISAPPEARED AND THE HOPES OF THE NATION NOW REST ON THREE PAIRS OF GIGANTIC HAIRY SHOULDERS...

DEEP IN THE PACIFIC OCEAN, A COLOSSAL ARMY OF SEA MONSTERS IS RISING UP TO ATTACK THE WORLD.

WITH GIANT SQUID LAYING SIEGE TO COASTAL CITIES AND GLOBAL SEA DEFENSES IN RUINS, THERE ARE ONLY THREE CREATURES LEFT TO KEEP HUMANITY AFLOAT: THE YETIS OF THE MYTHICAL 9TH DIVISION.

COMING SOON
THE ALIEN MOON

DON'T MISS THE
NEXT AMAZING MISSION